# JORAN

STAR-CROSSED ALIEN MAIL ORDER BRIDES

SUSAN HAYES

# ABOUT THE BOOK

*What do you do when your planet runs out of women? Send for takeout, of course.*

Joran, Crown Prince of Pyros, needs to claim his mate in order to ascend to the throne one day. The problem? His destined mate isn't on Pyros.

When a galaxy-wide search uncovers a backwater world full of potential mates for Joran and the other unmated males on his planet, plans are set in motion and Star-Crossed Dating is created. Now, the first wave of men are on their way to claim their unsuspecting brides. Joran's mission: Go to Earth, claim his mate and bring her back to Pyros. How hard could it be?

This book contains a redheaded barista who doesn't believe in aliens, and a prince who is used to getting anything he wants without having to work for it...until now.

# COPYRIGHT

ALL RIGHTS RESERVED: This literary work may not be reproduced or transmitted in any form or by any means, including electronic or photographic reproduction, in whole or in part, without express written permission.

All characters and events in this book are fictitious. Any resemblance to actual persons living or dead is strictly coincidental. It is fiction so facts and events may not be accurate except to the current world the book takes place in.

# DEDICATION

*For my Mum and Dad, for supporting me even when they thought I was crazy. And for my best friend, Karen, for putting up with me when I was definitely nuts.*


*This book is also dedicated to Violet V for inviting me to join this series. I had a blast writing this story, thank you!*

Maggie nestled into one side of her best friend's worn but comfy couch with a container of rocky road ice cream in one hand and a spoon in the other. After the week she'd had, ice cream and a girls' night in was exactly what she needed.

"Do we want to open the red or white wine?" Gwen called from the tiny, galley-style kitchen.

"Red. That's a good pairing for cookie dough ice cream, right?" Lisa said, already digging into her ice cream from her perch on the other side of the couch.

"Everything's a good pairing for cookie dough." Gwen reappeared with a bottle of red wine and three glasses on a tray, along with her preferred flavor, chocolate ripple.

Gwen served the wine and then settled into a somewhat battered armchair with a contented sigh and raised her glass. "We survived another week. Here's to the weekend."

"Amen," Maggie replied, before downing a significant portion of her glass.

"Uh oh. You only drink your wine that fast when the espresso machine at work is on the fritz or you're having man trouble. Which is it?"

Maggie wrinkled her nose and sighed. "The latter. Jorge went back to his wife."

Gwen's hand froze, her spoon hovering halfway between the carton and her mouth. "Wife? I thought you said he was divorced?"

"He is. Well, he was. They finalized the divorce three years ago." Maggie took another drink, but the wine couldn't wash away the bitter taste that had lingered in her mouth since she got the text from Jorge the night before.

"Weren't you two planning a romantic getaway next weekend? How the hell does a guy go from booking a trip with his girlfriend to getting back together with his ex-wife?" Lisa leaned over to snag the bottle of wine off the table and refilled Maggie's glass.

"It was his turn with the kids last weekend. I guess he told them about me, and they went home and told their mother." Maggie paused to take another spoonful of ice cream while Lisa and Gwen reacted like the best friends that they were.

"He's an idiot. She doesn't want him back, she

just wants to make sure he isn't with anyone else. The moment she finds out he dumped you, she'll call it off again. If he can't see that, he's not worthy of you," Gwen said, utterly indignant.

"Please, tell me you had a moment of glorious red-headed temper and tore him a new one before punting his sorry ass to the curb," Lisa added.

"He didn't give me the chance. He told me by text message late last night."

"He broke up with you by *text*? The least he could have done was tell you in person. What kind of man does that?" Gwen asked.

"The only kind of man the three of us ever seem to attract. Weak, selfish assholes." Lisa stabbed her spoon into her ice cream. "We need to expand our dating pool."

Maggie shook her head. "I'm not sure how we'd do that. I work in a coffee shop, which means the only guys I meet are over-caffeinated business types who never look up from their phones long enough to flirt. You're a street artist, so you're surrounded by buskers all day. Those guys barely make rent, they can't afford a girlfriend."

Lisa grinned. "No, but the cute ones can rent me for a couple of days. Not every relationship has to last forever."

Gwen rolled her eyes. "Some of us are getting too old to play the field. I'd like to meet someone special. He doesn't need to be perfect, just...perfect for me."

"You've spent too many years reading those romance novels you love, Gwen. There's no such thing as a perfect man. He's a myth, like unicorns and little green men from outer space." Maggie took another drink of her wine. "I agree with Lisa though, we do need to find a better class of men to date. There has to be some out there, somewhere."

"Given our track records, maybe not. Between us, we've dated a card-carrying member of the Ghostbusters fan club, complete with his own proton pack, two guys who forgot they were still married..."

Gwen chimed in with "Don't forget the guy who met Lisa for coffee, talked about himself for an hour, then told her she was clearly a submissive and asked her to wear his collar...on their first date."

Lisa groaned. "Seth. Oh man, I'd forgotten about him. He was a wannabe Dom with no clue what he was talking about. Quick, someone pass me more wine. I'm going to need it to erase those memories again."

They spent the next hour drinking, laughing, eating ice cream, and reminiscing about their worst dating experiences. They'd been friends for so long they knew all the stories already, but that didn't matter. They still laughed at each other and tossed in the occasional reminder about a detail someone had missed. Usually something that made the whole tale even more humiliating. That's what friends were for.

Gwen and Lisa were more than friends, though. They were the sisters of her heart. They had been there for Maggie when she'd first landed in foster care as a broken and terrified twelve-year-old. Since then, the three of them had forged a friendship that had lasted twenty years.

"This might be the wine talking, but I think I'm ready to try online dating again," Lisa announced. "It's that or dye my hair. Whichever. It's time for a change."

"You have gorgeous hair. Do you know how many women would kill to be natural blondes?" Gwen tugged on a curl of her tightly spiraled, jet-black hair to make her point. "Me, for one."

"Then I'm taking your comment as a vote for a return to online dating. And so we're clear, I'm not going alone. You two are coming with me." Lisa grabbed her phone and started poking at the screen. "I got this email the other day. Some new dating site is coming online in the next few months, and they're looking for some brave souls to beta test it for free. Maybe we should give it a shot."

Maggie groaned. "You say that like you're going to give us a choice."

Lisa waved her hand around in vague circles. "What, and spoil the illusion? I like to let you guys think you have some say."

"We've been friends too long. That illusion got shattered years ago." Gwen drained her glass and then reached for her phone. "I can't believe I'm even considering this."

"Me, either." Maggie checked her email and quickly found the invite. Star-Crossed Dating Service.

A quick scan of the contents made her curious enough to click the link. The site looked professional enough. No spelling mistakes or weird links. She started to read, then stopped and read the same sentence over again.

"Am I reading this right? They offer a money back guarantee? If we're still single after six months, we get double our money back? I thought you said this was free?"

"Keep reading. In the next paragraph, they promise to pay us the cash, even as beta testers. They've got to be pretty confident to make that kind of offer," Lisa said.

"There has to be a catch." Gwen's expression darkened as she kept reading. "Young women looking for adventure and an out of this world dating experience. I'm not that young anymore, and I'm not sure I'm the adventurous type."

"You're thirty-four, not eighty. Come on, Gwen. Maybe your perfect-for-you guy is on this site, waiting to meet you. You'll never know unless you try." Lisa turned her gaze to Maggie. "So, what's your argument going to be?"

"I'm working on it. Give me a minute. I've had

enough wine and ice cream that it's tough to think right now."

"Perfect. In that case, have another glass." Lisa held up the nearly empty wine bottle. "Drink up, then sign up. We're doing this."

"Bossy cow," Maggie muttered with a laugh as she held out her glass.

"Mooo 'betcha," Lisa retorted, and all three of them burst into a fit of giggles.

The laughter continued as they filled out the questionnaire for the dating site, each of them offering up suggestions on what the others should put. It was certainly more fun than doing it alone, but Maggie still didn't expect much in the way of results. When it came to dating, being skeptical kept her from getting her hopes dashed over and over again.

As a girl, she'd lived like a princess in a fairytale, but when her father died, she'd lost everything. Her friends. Her home. Even her mother. She'd learned her lesson. Now, Maggie kept her expectations low and her dreams small. It was safer that way. If this dating site was as good as it claimed to be, then maybe it would match her with a man who under-stood how to live the same way she did. Small and simple.

Joran Pyr, Crown Prince of Pyros, was convinced his parents had lost their flaming minds. He stopped pacing the length of the ornate meeting room and spun on his heel to face them, turning his back on the portraits of his ancestors that lined the walls. "You're telling me that you ordered our pilots to use a rift generator--technology we're not supposed to have--to travel to the uncharted quadrants of our galaxy-- a place we aren't supposed to go. And the reason for this illicit jaunt across the cosmos is to look for potential mates on planets we're forbidden to interfere with because they're not advanced enough yet? What happens if the other members of the Inter-Planetary Council find out?"

"If they find out, we'll be at war. So, I suggest you lower your voice before someone overhears your dramatic recital of facts we'd all like to keep secret," his father, King Janus, replied.

"Mother, you went along with this?"

Lilanna nodded. "You need a mate, Joran. Since the one you're destined for is not on our planet, we've expanded the search."

Well, that confirmed it. They *were* insane. "You're risking an intergalactic war because you want grandchildren?"

"Yes," his mother replied.

"You're the last of our line, Joran. If you don't mate and produce an heir, the throne, and the fate of our planet, will pass to the House of Tindor." His father gestured to the rows of portraits that filled the space. "You were born to rule, and by the Flames of the First One, I will do everything I can to ensure you claim the throne when the time comes."

"If it was my destiny to rule, don't you think the Gods might have provided me with a mate? It's not like they don't know how this works. They made the rules, after all. No ruler may ascend the throne unless they have found their mate and undergone the Scorching. That's not going to happen when there are six males to every female on the damned planet." Joran uttered a bitter laugh. "If the Gods wanted your child to rule, maybe they should have given you a daughter."

His mother's golden eyes narrowed. "Or maybe you should give them more credit, son. Perhaps they brought about the lack of female births to force our people to search the stars. We were explorers once, and it may be that the Gods think it's time that we returned to the old ways again."

He loved his mother, but her faith in the Gods and their plans were beyond his understanding. Whenever he questioned her on it, she would smile and tell him that when he found his mate, he would understand.

*When he found his mate.* It was such a simple statement. Too bad reality was far more complicated. At first, the shift was so subtle no one noticed that there were more males than females being born.

Even once the trend was spotted, it was dismissed as an anomaly. By the time the pattern was obvious, it was too late. Fewer females meant fewer matings, which meant fewer babies born. The population of Pyros was caught in a diminishing cycle no one had been able to correct.

"It's still a terrible risk." Once, the Pyrosians were one of the most influential races in the quadrant. They commanded fleets of spaceships carrying thousands of warriors, including many males and females who had undergone the Scorching. With their flame manipulation powers unlocked, they were a force to be reckoned with. As the number of mated pairs diminished, so did the strength of their military. The council no longer bowed to their wishes. Instead, Pyros was forced to bow to others.

"And if we don't take the chance now, it might never come again." His father squared his shoulders and Joran braced for yet another lecture. He'd been on the receiving end of so many over the years, he had them all memorized. "We stand on the brink, son. The future of our people is at stake. You need to mate and have children. We need to rebuild, so that one day we can retake our place at the head of the council. When you sit in my place, you will learn that there are no easy choices."

"Besides, we aren't only doing this for you. If the Gods are generous, then we will find mates for others. I am not the only mother who fears her child will be the last of their line."

*Are those tears in her eyes?* Joran couldn't believe it. His mother was too strong for tears. Too practical to ever let emotions cloud her judgment. Queen Lilanna was the steadfast star around which the entire planet orbited. To see her unguarded and emotional was a comet strike to the heart.

He sat in one of the chairs across from his parents, and a heavy weight settled on his shoulders. Talking about the day he took the throne always made him feel this way. He'd been trained since birth to rule. That wasn't the problem. It was the fact that to claim the crown, he'd have to bury his father, first. What had once been a distant notion was now an unavoidable truth. His father was aging, and the added burden of trying to save his people was only accelerating the process.

"How bad is it? For all of this to be necessary, things must be far worse than you've let everyone believe, including me."

His father ran a hand through his greying hair and sighed. "I'll send you the reports tonight. Until now, no one has seen them but the two of us. This has to remain a secret. When I said we were on the brink, I wasn't being dramatic. It's the truth."

Joran swiped at his own hair, vaguely aware that he was mirroring his father's actions. They were very much alike. Both blond and brown-eyed, at least until the Scorching had changed his father's eyes to gold. They were both warriors at heart, and equally stubborn. A trait that had brought them into conflict more than once.

"I wish you had told me sooner."

"There was nothing you could have done. We didn't—" Lilanna glanced at Janus. "*I* didn't want you to worry."

"According to Father, worrying is part of the job." Joran leaned forwards in his chair as a new thought occurred to him. "You're telling me now, though. Does that mean the scouts found something?"

The lines around Janus' eyes softened a little. "We believe so. In a distant part of the galaxy, there is a planet that harbors a race that appears to be compatible with ours. More than that, our scientists have detected traces of Pyrosian genes in their DNA."

"How is that even possible? We've never been to that part of the galaxy."

"According to our records, no." His mother agreed. "But our records are incomplete. Our best guess is that one of the missing colony ships from the Age of Expansion must have found its way to this planet. Its inhabitants call it Earth."

"So, what happens now? How long have we been observing them? Have we made contact yet? What are we prepared to offer the inhabitants in exchange? They'd most likely want advanced technology. Another thing we're not allowed to offer to less-advanced species." Joran was musing out loud as a myriad of thoughts and concerns raced through his mind. It took him a few minutes to notice that his parents were sitting in stony silence.

He stopped talking and waited for one of them to speak. It was an uncomfortably long wait, and the longer it stretched on, the more certain he was he wouldn't like whatever was coming next.

"We can't make official contact. There will be no negotiations. We've already initiated a plan to identify unmated females and screen them for potential matches using the same system we've created to find mates for the females of our race."

"And if we find matches, what then?"

"Then we send our males to claim their mates and bring them home to Pyros. The first trip will have to be limited to only a few males."

Joran frowned. "How will they be selected?"

"To ensure that we have the support we need, we'll have to give the first opportunity to those who can fund this mission, or have political influence we might need if we're discovered," his mother explained.

"So we're starting with the unmated sons of the elite? That's not going to sit well with the rest of our people."

His father sighed and nodded. "I know. If this is successful, then we will open the matching process to include the other males, but remember, we cannot secret enough females away to match every male on this planet. The human species is advanced enough to notice if we are not careful."

Joran didn't like any of this. Not the restrictions for his people, or the plan to do this without the consent of world involved. "Is there no other way?"

"No, son," his father said.

"If your mate is on that planet, then it is because the Gods have willed it to be so. Her destiny is here. You *must* find a way to convince her of that." Lilanna's hand landed sharply on the table to emphasize her last words.

"And if she doesn't agree with the will of the Gods?" Joran asked.

"Then you will bring her here by whatever means necessary, no matter what her feelings may be." his father declared in a tone that bordered on royal command.

Lilanna gasped. "Janus!"

"You know that's not our way, Father." Joran shook his head in defiance. "I'll go, because that is what needs to be done for the good of our people. But I will not abduct a female from her homeworld against her will. No Pyrosian male would force a female that way."

"We cannot save our future by stealing someone else's," Lilanna rebuked her husband gently.

"You're right, *seska,*" Janus said with a sigh. "But there is so much at stake."

"I know you only want what's best for our people, but it falls to our son to convince his mate to come to Pyros."

Janus lifted his gaze to stare at Joran. "The future of our people is in your hands, Joran. Don't fail us."

The weight of his father's words pressed down on him, but he nodded stiffly and rose from his chair. "I will not fail, Sire. If my mate is out there, I will bring her home."

He'd been raised to understand that his birthright required sacrifice. It was his duty to do what he must for the sake of the ones they ruled. Now, he had to hope that whoever his mate was, she would forgive him for the sacrifices she was about to make in the name of a world she didn't know existed.

**2**
_______

When Maggie first saw the acceptance email in her inbox, she couldn't remember what it was for. Two months had passed since she and the others had made their wine-enabled decision to sign up for Star-Crossed dating site. This was the first time she'd heard from them since.

"Welcome to the most stellar dating experience of your life." She read the email from beginning to end, skimming the hyperbole and enthusiastic promises until she got to the important information near the bottom. First came the legal disclaimers, followed by a link. "Start your dating adventure today."

She closed the email without clicking. Before she agreed to this insanity, she wanted to know if Lisa and Gwen had been accepted, too. She wasn't going on this _adventure_ alone.

Almost immediately, her cell phone rang, the opening notes of Queen's "Bohemian Rhapsody" announcing the caller's identity. Lisa must have gotten an email, too. That's the only reason she'd call during Maggie's all too brief lunch break.

"Hi, Lisa. Let me guess, you got an acceptance letter from that dating site, too?"

There was a high-pitched shriek of excitement. "Oh my god. Yes! You got one too? Who did you get as your match? My guy is gorgeous. His name is Vadir, and he is stunning. I might have licked my screen."

"You clicked the link? I haven't done that, yet."

Maggie had to pull the phone away from her ear as Lisa's voice hit a note that made her wince and probably sent every dog within earshot running for cover.

"Do it!"

"My break is nearly over. I should probably wait—"

"No waiting. Do it now. Put me on speaker and tell me who they matched you with. If you don't, I'll come by this afternoon and pester you while drinking nothing but double shot Americanos."

"You wouldn't do that to me." Lisa was high-energy on a normal day. Lisa highly caffeinated was something out of a science fiction novel. You could almost see her vibrating fast enough to move through solid matter.

"You know I would. Now open that email again before I decide to start sketching nudes and give them all your face."

"Clicking. I'm clicking!" Maggie fumbled with her phone for a few seconds, but eventually, she managed to put Lisa on speaker and call up the email again. She hit the button and waited for the site to reveal what they promised would be her perfect match.

"Well?"

"Waiting on the Wi-Fi. Hang on."

A name appeared first, along with a few descriptive tidbits. Her match's name was Joran, and he was six feet tall with blond hair, brown eyes and...holy shit, was that his picture?

Lisa laughed. "Is he hot?"

"Huh?"

"You just cursed out loud when you saw his photo. So, what does he look like?"

Maggie wasn't sure how to describe the man on her screen. Hot didn't begin to cover it. His hair was trimmed short at the sides, but longer at the top, falling in soft waves around his forehead. He had a chiseled jaw, perfect cheekbones, and a boyishly charming smile that probably caused women to fall at his feet on a regular basis.

"It has to be a fake photo. No one that good looking could possibly need a website to get a date."

"If my guy is half as yummy in person, I'm calling it a win."

"You've already decided to meet your match? Isn't that a little...fast?" Maggie asked.

"You know me. I like to move past the awkward email conversations as quickly as possible. You can't tell what a guy is really like until you're face-to-face. That's the only real way to know if there's any chemistry. Besides, we've come this far, why not meet these guys? I bet Gwen got someone amazing, too. Why don't you spend the last few minutes of your break reading up on your match, while I call Gwen and see how she did?"

Maggie agreed and hung up. She had less than five minutes left before she had to go back to work, and she wanted to take the time to read the rest of Joran's profile. Lisa might believe in chemistry, but she also believed in crystal therapy, crop circles, and UFO's. Maggie preferred to be more pragmatic. If something appeared too good to be true, it usually was.

By closing time Maggie still hadn't found any reason to reject Joran out of hand. Of course, he hadn't gotten in touch with her, either, so maybe he'd already rejected her as a match and moved on to the next one. Vancouver was full of beautiful, single women. It didn't make any sense that he'd want to spend any time getting to know someone like her. She was so far out of his league they weren't even playing the same game.

She was cleaning up when the door chimes sounded. Jess must have forgotten to flip the sign over to closed on her way out. "I'm afraid we're closing down for the night. I can make you a cup of regular coffee to go if you'd like? And I think we've still got some orange and cranberry biscotti left," She called out without bothering to look up from her task.

"A regular coffee would be fine, thanks. And uh, what's a biscatti?"

A tingle raced down her spine as the customer spoke. She couldn't place his accent, but whatever it was, she liked it. A lot.

"Biscotti? If you don't know what that is, you can't be from around here." She popped up from behind the counter with a smile. "Where are you from? I've never heard your accent before and I...Joran?"

Standing at the serving counter in front of her was the man from the dating service. It had to be him. There couldn't be two men in the world who had won the same genetic lottery.

He was here. Now. He looked incredible, and she was in a shapeless uniform shirt, with her hair in a frizzy braid and only a minimal amount of makeup. The universe was seriously messing with her today.

"Do I know you?" he asked.

"I uh. No. I mean, sort of. We've never met though. I'm Maggie. I joined Star-Crossed dating service, and I'm pretty sure they sent me your profile a little while ago. How are you even here? I didn't list my work address."

"You're my match? Really? I haven't checked my email in a few hours. I was just roaming the city, exploring a little, and got thirsty. This is a coincidence, but I have to say, it's a very nice one." His smile brightened. "I'm Joran. Joran Pyr. It's nice to meet you, Maggie."

"Hi. I'm Maggie O'Hara." She reached across the counter and offered him her hand. This wasn't the way she'd hoped to meet her match for the first time, but she'd have to make the most of it. He only hesitated a second before taking her hand, coffee stains and all. The moment they touched, a blue spark crackled and arced from her hand to his. "Sorry. Must be static electricity."

***

Joran knew exactly what that Spark was, and it had nothing to do with static. She was the one. This green-eyed beauty with hair the colour of flame was his mate. He owed his mother, and the Gods, an apology.

"Uh, if you want coffee, I'm going to need my hand back."

"Sorry." He forced himself to let go when what he really wanted to do was pull her closer. If there hadn't been a counter between them, he probably would have. He needed to have her near him. Soon, that need would become an insatiable desire. The Scorching had begun.

He hadn't considered that possibility when he'd decided to come down to Maggie's workplace. He'd been staring at her image every day since the match had been confirmed, and he didn't want to wait any longer to see her. He'd been so focused on checking out the female he was supposed to bring home to Pyros, he'd given no thought to what might happen if they touched. Until it happened, he hadn't been sure this human female could even trigger a full mating bond. Apparently, she could.

"Do you want anything in your coffee?"

The question confused him. What else did humans put in their coffee beside coffee? There hadn't been enough time to create a complete database of every language and culture on this diverse planet. He and the half-dozen other matched males had all undergone cognitive augmentation to learn what they could, but now he was here, Joran was quickly realizing how much he didn't know. "What would you recommend?"

"How about a shot of vanilla syrup?"

"That sounds good." He had no idea what vanilla was. He'd never had coffee, either, for that matter, but now wasn't the time to worry about it. He had bigger problems. Like inadvertently triggering a mating bond before he and his off-world mate had exchanged more than a few words of greeting. This wasn't how he'd imagined things would go. Flames and fury, he hadn't actually believed this could happen. They weren't even the same species! Oh, she had some Pyrosian DNA in her cells. The scans had confirmed that much. But knowing the science was one thing. Seeing the Spark arc between them was another matter entirely.

This wasn't the plan others had laid out for him. He was supposed to make contact through the archaic communication protocol the humans called email, put Maggie at ease, and then arrange a meeting at one of the pre-selected locations. Somewhere without witnesses or surveillance equipment, like the security cameras this establishment had. He was also supposed to stay in contact with the main ship and keep at least one member of the royal guard with him at all times. He wasn't good with plans. His communicator was currently turned off, and he'd ditched his guards on the way here. They'd find him eventually, but for the moment, he was alone with the woman he'd crossed a galaxy to find.

She handed him a mug of something, and he managed to brush his fingers across the back of her hand before she moved away. There was no spark this time, just a rush of heat and raw desire that hit him like a plasma charge.

"I need to grab your biscotti." She blushed, and her eyes widened. "Oh, god. I meant I'll go get the rest of your order. I'm so sorry. That came out wrong."

She bolted into the back of the café before he could say anything, which was probably a good thing. He was tempted to tell her she could grab any part of him she wanted to. Flame and fury, if this was what the next few hours were going to be like, he was going to have to hurry up and explain matters before he lost his mind completely.

He laid down some currency on the counter to cover his order, then took out his phone. He'd acquired one as part of the ruse to make him appear human. He logged into the dating site his people had created and called up her profile. She had no idea he had memorized every detail already, including quite a few facts that she hadn't included in her application. He knew so much about her, and none of it had prepared him for this moment.

He was still staring at his phone when she reappeared.

"I looked at what we had left and decided to upgrade you to one of our wildberry muffins. They're delicious, and the berries are all local and organic."

The scent of the sweet confection blended with

her natural perfume, making his senses reel. "Thank you." He held up the device and showed her the screen so she would see what he'd been doing. "I thought I'd check your profile. They seem pretty confident we're a good match."

"Yeah, they do. But that's just a computer's calculation. You can't really be sure until you meet someone." She blushed again, her pale skin turning a charming shade of pink.

"I think the computer got it right. I'd like to take you out and spend more time with you." He took a sip of the brew in his mug and waited for her response.

She laughed and looked at him with disbelief. "You want to go out with me? Why?"

He had no idea how to answer that. She was his destined mate. He would never want any other female except her, and she was questioning why he wanted to spend time with her?

"Because I think we're destined for each other." It wasn't the whole truth, but it was as close as he could get without sending her into a panic.

"Because a computer program said so?" She gestured to herself with a dismissive flick of her hand. "I'm nothing special. We've barely said a dozen words to each other. So, tell me why you think we're fated to be together?"

He was going to have to lie and hope for forgiveness later. "I walked in here to get something to drink, and you recognized me on sight. I hadn't even looked up your profile yet. That's destiny."

Her lips curved up into a faint smile. "Okay, you might have a point there."

"So, that's a yes?"

Her smile got a little warmer. "It's a maybe. I need to finish cleaning and lock up. You can stay until I'm done. Then I'm going home. I'll give you my answer then."

"Is it close enough that I can walk with you?" He knew she lived only a short distance away, but he wasn't going to admit that to her. That would fall into the category of stalking, something he'd read about in his research. Stalking was a practice that didn't exist on his world, where every female was treated with care and consideration. It was, apparently, a common problem on Earth. This really was a primitive planet. His mate wasn't safe here. The sooner he got her on the ship back to Pyros, the better.

---

"You want to walk me home?" Maggie asked, not bothering to hide her surprise. The last time a guy had offered to walk her home, she'd been in high school.

"I do." He gave her another charming smile.

"Now that we've met, I don't have any plans on letting you out of my sight for a while."

She was doing her best to keep her hopes in check, but the more Joran spoke, the more she liked him. "Tell me something about yourself while I finish up. I'll decide about the escort when it's time to go." She paused and then pointed to his untouched muffin. "And I promise you, that is worth every sinful calorie. Eat up."

His eyes widened, and the smile vanished as his mouth fell open. She thought he was going to take offense, but instead, he burst out laughing and broke off a portion of the muffin. "As you wish, my lovely match."

She turned away to hide her face as she turned several shades of red. He was flirting with her. Guys who looked that good in a simple collared shirt and blue jeans didn't flirt with her unless they wanted something. As far as she could tell, there was absolutely nothing this man could need from her. Not unless he was planning on hiring his own personal barista, and no one could afford that kind of expense unless he was rich...dammit. She needed to look at his profile again and figure out what was going on.

"This tastes incredible. What did you say this fruit was called again?"

"There are raspberries and blueberries in there. Don't tell me you've never had raspberries before?

Where are you from that you don't have berries and biscotti?"

"I'm new here. In fact, I've only been in town a short time. I'm still getting used to all the differences."

"Moving is always hard. It takes some time to settle in, but before you know it, you'll feel like you've been here your whole life. Trust me, I've moved around enough to know." There was an ugly stretch of time between the time her dad died and when the system declared her mother unfit. They moved around constantly while her mom spiraled deeper and deeper into her booze-soaked depression.

"This is the farthest I've ever been from home."

There was a hint of longing in his voice. Wherever home was, he must have someone there that he cared about. "So, you signed up with this dating site to meet new people in your new city?" Something that felt alarmingly like jealousy sank its needle-sharp claws into her heart. She didn't want him to meet anyone else. She wanted to keep him all to herself. Her brain slammed to a screeching halt that sent her thoughts derailed in a tangled mess. Jealous? What the hell? She'd known Joran less than ten minutes. They hadn't been out on a single date. How could she be possessive about a man she barely knew?

"My mother talked me into it. She hates the idea

of me spending my life alone. Having met you, I think I might need to thank her for the suggestion."

She looked up to find him staring at her in open admiration, and for a second she could have sworn his eyes gleamed gold. "Maybe wait until after we've been out before you call and thank her for anything."

That sexy mouth of his quirked up into a grin that made her heart do a backflip. "See? That didn't take you long to agree. You're feeling this, too."

"That wasn't— I mean, it was, but I hadn't meant to— And now I'm babbling again. Okay, we'll go out. But I need to go home and clean up, first."

"Of course. This is all very spontaneous for both of us. We'll have to figure things out as we go." He took a sip of his coffee, but his gaze never wavered. He watched her with an intensity that should be disturbing but wasn't. For some reason, she liked being the focus of his attention.

"I'm not good with spontaneous. I usually like to have things planned out." She wiped down the last of the equipment and went over to the cash register. I'll be back in a few minutes. Enjoy your coffee."

She took the money from the till and carried it to the back. Her boss liked to balance the books and cash out the day's earnings herself, so all Maggie had to do was set everything in the safe and lock it up for the night.

She pulled out her phone and sent a hurried text

to Lisa and Gwen letting them know she had a date and would explain later. Then she looked up Joran's profile again. If she was going out with the man, it would help a little if she had some idea where he was from and what he did for a living.

There wasn't a whole lot to go on. He'd listed Vancouver as his current address, and his profession was listed as Vice-President of Project Development with a salary of— she nearly dropped her phone in shock. He made more in a month than she did in a year. This had to be some sort of elaborate hoax or scam. Either that, or Joran was the real thing.

Did this mean dragons were real, too?

## 3

Joran checked his other communication device while Maggie was out of the room. As he expected, he had several messages from his guards, and one from Kash Denza, the commander of the *Firebrand*, the ship that had brought them here. Commander Denza was threatening to come down in person if Joran didn't check in soon.

He grinned. Kash had been Joran's commanding officer during his mandatory stint in the Pyrosian military. He was one of the few people who dared to bark orders at the Crown Prince.

It was too risky to use verbal communication, so Joran tapped out a message in military shorthand. "Located target. Verified compatibility. Will initiate extraction when possible."

The message would probably send Kash into orbit. His job was to ensure that Joran was safe and that both Joran and Vadir's retrieval missions went smoothly. In the beginning, a member of the planning committee had suggested luring the females to a meeting place and abducting them without the males they were destined for even being present. It would mean far less risk to the males, but he and his mother had quickly put an end to that idea. These females might not be the same species, but they would still be treated with respect and integrity. If this plan was going to work, it would be because each female *chose* to go with her match.

He put away his communicator and settled in to enjoy his coffee and muffin. It was a shame that Earth was generations away from being ready to join the other intelligent species in the galaxy. They had an abundance of resources and unique foodstuffs that would have been welcomed on the interstellar market. Vadir ran an interstellar trading business. He would be sorely tempted by all the untapped trade potential here.

There were still a few bites of his snack remaining when Maggie reappeared, and he forgot about the food, markets, and his fellow Pyrosians. She'd undone the braid that held her hair back and it fell around her shoulders in fiery red waves. He wanted to tangle the weight of it in his fingers and use it to pull her in close enough he could finally have her in his arms.

He'd had his share of women in his life. His

wealth and power attracted them even when they knew they could never be his queen. He'd enjoyed their company, and the pleasure they'd shared, but he had never craved them the way he did Maggie.

"I need to pop your stuff in the dishwasher, then we can go."

"Allow me." He rose from his seat and picked up his dishes.

"Customers aren't supposed to be in the back area."

"This establishment is closed, correct? As such, I can't be a customer. Besides, I think you've worked hard enough today. I don't want to start our evening off by having you wait on me."

Surprised flared in her green eyes, and it made him wonder how many people in her life had treated her like a servant before she stopped expecting anything else.

With nothing more than a nod, she gestured for him to follow her past the counter and into the preparation area. Once the dishes were dealt with, he followed her back out again. He jammed his hands into his pockets to keep from reaching for her until they were outside. The moment she locked the door, he took her hand in his and asked, "So, which way do we go?"

"My friends and I have a little place not far from here." She pointed down the street, then gave an experimental tug on her hand. He didn't let go, and she frowned slightly but didn't pull away again.

"Friends? You share a place?" The file he had on her stated she lived alone.

"In this city? Unless you're rich, you pretty much have to have someone to share expenses with if you want to be able to afford the necessities of life, like food and clothing. We're not really roommates, though. More like neighbours. The house we have is split into three separate living areas."

"So you have your friends close, but still have your privacy." It wasn't that different from the way he lived back on Pyros. The royal family all lived in the palace, but he had his own suite of rooms. It concerned him that she had close friends, though. The objective was to select females who had no family or ties to this planet. That was part of the filtering process. At least, it was supposed to be.

She gave him an odd look, then started walking. "Exactly. I didn't expect someone like you to understand that."

"Someone like me?" He wasn't sure what she meant by that, but he didn't feel like it was any kind of compliment.

"I read your profile. You're rich. And you have a job that ensures everyone around you has to do as you say. Your life is very different from mine."

He stopped walking, perplexed by her response. Most females he'd met liked him because of who he was, and what he could provide them with. "I'm rich, yes. Why do you say that like it's a bad thing?"

Shadows darkened her eyes, the effect enhanced by the fact the sun vanished behind a fast moving band of dark clouds at the same moment.

"We're going to get caught in that rain squall if we don't move it." She said.

"Not until you answer my question."

She glowered at him and yanked her hand out of grasp. "My parents had money. Then my dad died, and that all went away. Being rich didn't protect us. People like you all share that same belief that somehow your money and influence will protect you. You live in your glass towers and look down on the rest of us, but the truth is you're as vulnerable to rocks as everyone else."

"Are rocks a common problem on this planet? Is there a threat from asteroids?" He didn't mean to say any of that out loud, but her declaration had him confused and irritated.

"It's an expression. You know, people who live in glass houses shouldn't throw stones. And what do you mean, on this planet? What other planets are there?"

"I'm not familiar with that expression. And I don't like being judged by the actions of others. If you're going to condemn me, let it be for the things I've said and done, not anyone else." Fire streaked through him as he reached for her and caught her hands in his. He hauled her in close, beyond caring about protocols, plans, or risks.

"What do you think you're doing?" she demanded as he locked one arm around her and speared his fingers into her hair with his other hand.

"What I've wanted to do since the first time we touched." He dropped his head and kissed her. Once their mouths met, there was no turning back for him. The Scorching roared to full strength and burned away every other thought in his head. This was his mate, and he needed to claim her.

Her lips were sweeter than the confection she'd offered him, the scent and taste of her more delicious than anything he'd ever experienced. Her very essence was being imprinted on his senses, locking them together for the rest of their lives. When this day was done, she would be the only female he would ever desire. She would complete him in every way. This was the moment that would start their new life together, and she wasn't even aware of it, yet. He needed to tell her.

Joran lifted his head to explain, but he didn't get a single word uttered before Maggie slapped him hard enough to make him see sparks.

"Let go of me! Now, or I swear I'll smack you again."

She'd hit him. This fierce little human that barely came to his shoulder had actually struck him, the prince of Pyros. He released her and grinned, ignoring the lingering sting where she'd connected. "No one has ever dared to do that before, but if that is the price for kissing you, lovely human, then by all means, strike me again."

Maggie took several scrambling steps backwards and then glared at him again. "Buddy, I don't know where you're from, but around here, kissing any woman without her permission is going to get you slapped. If this is the way you're going to behave, then our date is off."

She was canceling their date? No! She couldn't refuse him. Not now. "You're mine, Maggie O'Hara. You can't walk away from me."

"Like hell I can't!" She spun on her heel and marched away from him, head high.

She'd only gone a few paces before the rain started. It went from a shower to a pelting torrent in a matter of seconds, and the cool water helped him regain his wits, at least for a few minutes. It wouldn't be long before the mating drive overwhelmed him again. He needed to catch up to his runaway mate and explain matters, and there was only one place he could make sure she stayed long enough to hear him out: his shuttle.

He took off after her, his fingers already coding in the emergency extraction command into the tele-porter he wore on his wrist. It was only good for short distances and it wasn't the most comfortable form of travel, but it was the only option he had.

She should have known Joran was too good to be true. He might look like sex on a stick, but he had a screw or two loose. He'd called her a lovely human and asked about *this* planet. Like he'd come from another one. And who did he think he was, telling her she *belonged* to him? She was a grown woman, not a possession.

Tears of anger stung her eyes and blended with the rainwater already on her cheeks. She had actually been stupid enough to think that maybe this was going to be something incredible. That the dating service had actually paired her with someone she could fall for. There was something about him. And that kiss...

She shook her head as if that would somehow clear her head and muttered, "He's not worth crying over."

"You're crying?" A hand landed on her shoulder, the grip gentle but still firm enough to make her stop.

"Yes. No. It's just the rain. Why are you following me, Joran? I thought I made it clear we're done." She turned around to face him and nearly swayed into his arms when a sudden bout of dizziness hit her.

"I've made a flaming mess of this. I'm sorry." He reached up to stroke his thumb across her wet cheek. "I promise, I'll make this up to you."

"You're not going to get a chance to. I'm going home, and you're not coming with me."

He sighed and shook his head, sending fresh trickles of rainwater down his face. "We're going home together."

Before she could react, he slipped his hand from her cheek to the back of her head as he closed the last step that separated them. There was a high pitched squeal that drove itself deep into her bones and then absolute silence. Like a thunderclap of nothingness. She couldn't feel her own body. God, she couldn't sense anything at all. No sound. No light. Joran was gone, too. She was alone in some endless void.

Time passed, but she couldn't tell how much. A second? An hour? Then suddenly, the world came rushing back. Light, noise, touch, even the sound of her heartbeat hit with the force of a tidal wave. A scream tore from her throat, a blend of terror and relief as her body caught up with her senses.

"It's okay, Maggie. It's over. You can add that to the list of things I'm going to have to make up to you in the years to come."

Joran's comment cut through her disorientation like a laser. "What the hell did you do to me and what do you mean, the years to come? We're not spending years together, you asshole. We're not spending two more minutes together. Let me go!"

She started to fight, only to stumble backwards

when he did as she asked and let go. Still shaky from whatever the hell he'd done to her, she did an ungainly scramble, regained her balance and turned her back on him. She was going home. Her foot froze in mid-step as she finally took in her surroundings. They weren't on the street anymore. Hell, they weren't even outside.

Smooth walls painted pale cream. Tiled floors that glowed faintly gold and orange. A panel, lit with scrolls and squiggles she didn't recognize. No door. No windows. Panic bloomed in her chest, gripping her heart and squeezing her lungs until she could barely breathe.

"Where? How?" she croaked her questions.

"We're onboard my ship. I brought us here so I could explain everything to you." Joran reappeared at her side, his left arm held out to show her something that looked like a bulky watch strapped to his wrist. "It's a teleporter."

"You teleported us here? As in, blip, poof, presto, we're somewhere else now? Wait, did you say ship?" She didn't want to believe him, but it was hard to argue with the evidence. She was still soaked to the skin from the rainstorm, and the water was starting to pool on the strange, glowing floor. They were definitely not outside anymore.

"I don't understand everything you said, but yes. We're on my shuttle, several miles away from where we were before."

She folded her arms across her chest, as much to hide their shaking as to express her anger. "Take me back."

"I can't do that. Not yet." Joran gave her a look of frustration and regret. "Once I've explained, you'll probably still be angry at me, but at least you'll understand."

"You bet I'm angry at you! You kidnapped me."

"I claimed my mate," he retorted, his eyes flashing gold again. This time they stayed that colour long enough she knew it wasn't a trick of the light. What the hell had she gotten herself into?

"I'm not your anything. I'm sure as hell not your mate." She spat out the last word with all the venom she could muster, but even as she said it, something inside of her clamored in denial.

Instead of arguing he held out his hand. "Come with me."

*Yes. Go with him.* That traitorous little voice inside her heart spoke again, louder this time. "No. Not until you explain."

"Maggie, please. I need to show you that I'm telling you the truth. There's nothing in this airlock that I can use to convince you, so we need to go to another part of the ship."

If he let her out of here, maybe she'd be able to figure out how the doors worked. She was going to need that information to escape. Not that she believed she was on a ship. This was all some elaborate ruse. It had to be. "Fine. You lead. I'll follow. No touching."

"If that is your wish, my *seska*." Joran gave her a small smile and moved towards the panel on the wall. He waved his hand near a small, red light, and part of the wall vanished, forming a doorway.

"What's a *seska*?" she asked as she followed him through the doorway.

He chuckled, and somehow the bastard made it sound sexy. "If I tell you, you're going to be angrier than you already are. Ask me again once I've explained things."

"Do you really think explaining why you abducted me is going to help calm me down?"

"Probably not, but I still owe you that much. Hurry, we don't have a lot of time left."

"Before the police come looking for me?"

He glanced back at her. "No, *seska*. Before the Scorching hits us both so hard, we'll be beyond words."

The list of questions she wanted answers to was getting longer by the minute. The odd thing was, she was having a hard time staying mad. She'd always used her anger like a shield. It was easy to be angry when you'd lost as much as she had. But now, when she needed to keep her guard up, she had to fight to remember why she was upset. Joran was here, and he would take care of her...

No! She gave herself a mental slap. Joran was the reason she was in this mess in the first place.

She followed Joran down a bland looking corridor. He was right about one thing, there wasn't anything in sight that screamed "spaceship." She kept looking around, doing her best to ignore the trickles of water that chased down her back and dripped into her eyes. Even her shoes squelched with every step she took. Despite her sodden state, she wasn't feeling chilled at all. Wherever they were, the temperature must be downright tropical. "I don't suppose we could stop for a towel on the way?"

"I can do better than that." He stopped speaking English and lapsed into a language that sounded nothing like she'd ever heard before. His tone sharpened, the syllables snapping and cracking as they rolled off his tongue.

"What was that?"

"I ordered the ship's computer to send a service droid to bring some towels to the cockpit."

"In what language? Klingon?"

He was smiling at her now. "That was the language of my people. I promise, your answers are coming."

"They'd better be. And if you're giving orders to imaginary robots now, maybe you could get them to turn down the heat a bit? It's too hot in here."

He turned around so fast she walked right into him. "When did that feeling start?"

"I don't know. Since we got here?"

"I never imagined this would happen so quickly. Flames, I never really thought it could happen at all. I'm sorry, Maggie."

He held out his hand, and this time she took it. She hadn't intended to, but it happened anyway. "You're not making any sense. I'm trying to be reasonable here, but you abducted me, and you keep saying things I don't understand."

He pulled her in close, but instead of kissing her again, he hugged her and buried his face in her wet hair. "Here's the truth, *seska*. My name is Joran Pyr, and I am not from your world. We're safe on my shuttle, and we need to stay here until the Scorching has passed. You are my mate, Maggie O'Hara. I have crossed the galaxy to find you and bring you home."

For the first time since Joran had walked into her life, she was terrified. Not because of any of the strange and insane things that had happened, but because she believed every word he'd just said.

Heat flared deep in her heart. Her pulse raced, and a fiery need flowed through her like molten metal. None of it made any sense. She was crazy to even think this was really happening, but she did. And that left only one question she needed him to answer. "Assuming I believe all this. Why would you come all this way? I'm nothing special."

Joran straightened and moved back so that he was looking down at her. "That's where you're wrong. My race doesn't date the way you humans do. We have only one mate, and when we find them, we claim them for life. Two souls, one destiny." He took her hand and interwove their fingers.

"I'm not your mate. How can I be? As you've pointed out several times now, I'm human, and you're...not." She tugged at her hand, but all he did was tighten his grip on her fingers.

"I am Pyrosian, and you *are* my mate. That Spark that arced between us the first time we touched wasn't a static discharge, it was a sign that we belong together."

"You kidnapped me over a spark?" disbelief made her voice crack.

"Yes. And because of what I've been feeling since that moment." He leaned in close enough that his breath caressed her face. "Don't try and tell me you don't know what I'm talking about. You can feel it too. The heat. The pulse-pounding need to touch. What we're feeling is called the Scorching. It's the mating fever."

She didn't bother denying what she was feeling. How could she when it was taking all her will to resist leaning in and kissing him. "How do we make it stop?"

"There is no stopping this. I regret that I touched you before I had a chance to explain matters, but that won't change the outcome. You're going to be mine, soon, and forever."

"Outcome? As in what? Marriage? Sex? Are we even compatible? What if you have two dicks or something?"

His laughter stoked the fire already burning inside her. "Marriage, yes. Sex, absolutely. And I hope a lot of it. As for being compatible..." he pulled her hand to his chest, then drew it slowly down until she could feel the hard ridge of an impressive erection under her fingers.

She ignored the blush that bloomed on her cheeks as she ran her hand down his length. It was quickly apparent that he wasn't wearing a damned thing under his pants, and it was all she could do not to undo them and take what he was so clearly offering. Maybe there was something to his talk about mating fever. Either that, or she was losing what was left her mind.

Why not? She'd already lost her inhibitions and her ability to filter anything that came out of her mouth. Might as well go for the trifecta.

"Okay, we're compatible. Maybe. And you're apologizing for touching me, but not for teleporting me to...are we really on a space ship? And where's this droid with our towels?" Her brain was flitting from topic to topic around faster than a humming-bird on a sugar high.

"Yes, we're on a space ship. The droid is waiting for us in the cockpit, but we're not going to make it that far. I had intended on showing you around, but I think that will have to wait until afterwards."

"After what?"

His eyes changed colour again. A flash of brilliant gold that made her breath lock in her throat and her heart race. "After we're mated."

"Not happening." She knew it was a lie the moment she uttered the words. She wanted him so badly it hurt.

"You know that isn't true."

"This can't be happening."

"This is real, Maggie. Believe it." His lips crashed down on hers, kissing her with so much heat she felt like her very soul had been seared.

The last shreds of her self-control burned up in the first seconds of that kiss, leaving her free to take what she needed. What she wanted. *Him.*

## 4

She rose up on her toes and kissed him back for the first time.

She'd accepted him.

Joran's world went up in flames. He wanted to drink in her essence and commit every detail to memory. The soft lilt of her voice, the whiff of coffee and sugar that clung to her skin, the taste and feel of her in his arms. He'd found her.

The mating drive flared hotter with every kiss and caress they shared. There was nothing in his experience that came close to this feeling. Primal need coursed through him, growing stronger by the second. He needed to touch, to taste, to hear her moans of pleasure as the Scorching took them both.

"Joran?" his name fell from her lips with soft, shuddering sigh.

"What do you need, *seska*?"

"You. I need you." She paused, and he could see her fighting to think through the fog of lust that was clouding both their minds.

"What else do you need?" It was hard to hold himself back, but he'd rushed her enough already. Whatever she needed to say, he would give her the time to say it.

"Promise me you won't hurt me. Ever."

"Never. You're my mate. My centre. I'd die before I let anything hurt you."

"Promise," she repeated, her eyes shadowed by doubt.

Words he'd once believed he would never say fell from his lips. "I vow by the Flames of the First One, to protect my mate—you, Maggie O'Hara, from all who would do her harm. She will be my Queen, my lover, and my most cherished companion from now until we return to the Flame that birthed us." As he finished, he realized he'd spoken his vow in Pyrosian, and he repeated them in English so that Maggie would understand.

There were tears in her eyes as he finished, and the smile on her face was one of bewildered joy. "Yes."

It wasn't a formal vow, but that wasn't important. All that mattered was that she'd agreed to be his mate.

"Take hold of me."

"Anywhere in particular?" she asked, her voice gone husky with need and emotion.

"My shoulders...for now. The tour of my ship will have to wait. I need you, Maggie."

She laughed, and the sound made his heart soar. As soon as she reached for him, he lifted her into his arms and jogged the rest of the way to his quarters. For a small ship, it felt like it took an eternity to reach the door. Especially when he had his arms full of his turned-on and eager mate. His hands might be busy holding her, but hers weren't, and she was putting them to good use. By the time he got inside his small cabin, his shirt was half undone, and Maggie was exploring his newly bared chest with gentle fingers. When she tweaked one of his nipples, he groaned a warning. She ignored him. Instead of stopping, she did it again, this time while nuzzling her lips over his ear.

So, his mate was feeling brave enough to be playful, now? Good. Then let the games begin. He lowered her to her feet and let her take her first look around. It wasn't the palatial bower she would have once they were home, but it was at least comfortable.

After a brief glance around, Maggie burst out laughing. "Somehow, I imagined your cabin to be less uh, opulent. You really are rich, aren't you? I mean, clearly there are some omissions and lies on your dating profile, mister I'm from another planet, but this is something else."

"Opulent? This? The bed is too small, the rugs are thin, and the furnishings are functional but hardly ornate." They were also made of fire resistant materials, a precaution his mother had insisted on.

She laughed harder. "Wait until you see my place, then you'll understand."

"When we return to Pyros, you will live in the palace with me."

"Palace?"

"Yes, *seska*. You are the mate of the Crown Prince of Pyros, where else would you live?"

She blinked at him, her sweet mouth opening and closing several times before she finally spoke. "You're a *prince*? Oh my god. I thought this was an insane match when you were just a rich corporate type. A human one. This is..."

Maggie swayed, and he raced to her, pulling her in close and holding her against his chest. Her heart was pounding so hard he could feel it as he held her.

"This is what we're destined for. All you have to do is believe in that." He tipped her head back and kissed her softly. "Trust me, Maggie."

"I must be crazy," she whispered before gifting him with a smile that made him feel like he was already a king. "Because I do."

---

Maggie's head was spinning. There was too much for

her to process. Too many questions. All she knew for sure was how she felt about Joran. She craved him like a drug. She couldn't get enough. But more than that, she trusted him. He'd promised to protect her, and he would. She knew it.

She let go of everything else. For now, Joran was all she needed.

"I need to see you. Feel you. Flames, I need to make you mine before I burn." He took her purse, set it aside and then pulled her shirt up, and she raised her hands so that he could strip it off of her.

He had his hands back on her body before the shirt hit the red-and-gold rug they were standing on. Strong arms curved around her body as he bent down to bury his face between her breasts. Her nipples hardened instantly, drawing up into diamond-hard nubs that ached for his touch.

She ran her hands through his hair, cradling his head as he worshiped her body and set her skin on fire with need. When he ran his tongue down the valley between her breasts, her clit started to throb in time with her heartbeat, and when he finally closed his mouth over her nipple and sucked, a jolt of lust ran through her. Drunk with need, she shifted her lower body until she could wrap one leg around his and press her aching pussy to the hard muscles of his thigh.

He groaned and sucked harder as she ground herself against him, using his tongue to lap and tease at her sensitive nubs until she was quivering and desperate for more.

"Joran," she breathed his name, not even sure what she wanted to say.

"Tell me what you need, *seska*."

"I need..." she closed her eyes, too embarrassed to know what to say.

He lifted his head from her breasts and turned to press a tender kiss to the inside of her wrist. "Never hesitate to tell me what you want. How can we learn about each other otherwise? Now, what do you want me to do to you, Maggie? Do you want my fingers, my cock, or my tongue?"

She cracked open one eye to look at the sensual god the universe had decided to gift her with and pushed her embarrassment aside. "Would it be greedy if I said all three?"

He chuckled, a deep, rumbling sound that rolled through her like the tolling of a bell. "No, it wouldn't be. It would tell me that the Gods chose a mate with a passion to match my own."

She reached out and brushed a finger over his stomach, just above the catch of his pants. "I think it's time I saw you, too."

"As my mate wishes." He stripped off his shirt first, then stood with his hands on his hips and a wicked smirk on his face as he posed for her inspection.

Holy hell. If he'd taken his shirt off first, she

might have had an easier time believing he was an alien. He was too perfect to be human. He was muscular without being bulky, and every line of his body could have been sculpted by a master artist. Dazed, she reached out to touch him. "Wow. Do the rest of the men on your planet look like you?"

"Not all, but many. We are a warrior race. Even the gentlest scholar trains long enough to be able to defend their family. He shrugged his broad shoulders, and she watched in fascination at the way his muscles shifted beneath his skin. "My duties include overseeing our military. If I didn't train with them, how could I command their respect?"

She really wanted to hear more about his duties, his rank, and his people, but it would have to wait. Her desires were too strong. Her need too great to ignore. She stroked her hand down his hard stomach and daringly undid the button at the top of his pants. It was the most brazen she'd ever been. "I want to see all of you."

"Together."

Her heart hammered as she nodded in agreement. She kept her eyes on him and moved when he did. She undid her jeans and slid them over her hips, removing her panties at the same time, peeling her clothes off and kicking them away. She watched as he bared his body to her, revealing even more perfection. His cock rose up from between his legs, thicker and longer than any guy she'd been with, but not by enough to worry her.

"Do I meet with your approval?"

His words startled her, and she answered without thinking. "Hell yes, I approve. Oh my god, do I approve." She looked up to find him staring at her, and a final flicker of doubt made her ask, "Do I?"

"You are perfection itself." He took her hand and led her to the sumptuous red and gold draped bed that claimed most of the space in the cabin. "Lie back and let me show you how much I like what I see."

She stretched out across the bed, sinking into the softest fabric she'd ever felt.

He sank to his knees at the edge of the mattress and placed his hands on her ankles. "Now this is a feast fit for a prince."

Joran knew exactly what he wanted, and now he had his mate naked, he intended to lay claim to every inch of her, starting with her pussy. He slid his hands up her legs, parting her soft thighs wide as he moved into position. He blew a breath across her already glistening folds, and she gasped, her hips lifting to offer herself to him.

He used his thumbs to part her folds and expose

the delicate bud of nerves his studies revealed would give her the most pleasure. He dipped his head and ran his tongue over the tiny pearl, the sweet taste of her almost as pleasurable as the keening cry of need that rose from her throat at his touch. Her eagerness spurred him on, and he dove in, working her with mouth and tongue in unison.

The research he'd read hadn't prepared him for this. Understanding the small differences in their biology was one thing, but to experience her passionate responses, to feel her buck and quiver at his touch, was intoxicating. If his fellow Pyrosians were blessed with mates as passionate and amazing as his, then the Gods had truly been generous.

Every touch taught him more about her body, and soon he had her shuddering on the brink of release. When he drew her entire clit into his mouth and bit down gently, she arched off the bed with a wild cry and came.

She was still flushed and breathless when he rose from between her thighs to join her on the bed. When she opened her arms to him, he almost fell into her embrace. Mouths mated. Breaths shared. Bodies pressed together from lips to thigh. Her soft limbs twined around his, and he rolled them both over until he was beneath her.

"Claim what is yours, mate."

Desire flashed in Maggie's eyes as she settled herself atop him. She braced one hand against the mattress and reached between them to grip his cock. "I want you."

She pumped his shaft several times and then guided him into position. Without a word, she leaned down to kiss him, her breasts brushing against his chest as she rolled her hips in a slow rocking motion that teased them both. Unable to hold back any longer, he speared his tongue into her mouth and arched his body off the bed, sliding his cock partway into her channel.

She hummed in pleasure and eased herself slowly down around him, surrounding him in her slick heat. Her body gave way to his, wrapping around him in a tight embrace that had them both moaning and shaking with need by the time he was fully sheathed.

"We are one." He breathed the final words of claiming.

"Yes, we are."

She rose up and flexed her inner walls around him, setting his blood on fire as a torrent of exquisite pleasure flooded him. It was intoxicating, and he knew the Scorching had him completely in its thrall. Maggie seemed to feel it too, because she uttered a low moan and bucked her hips, driving him deep inside.

He placed his hands on her hips, helping her to balance as the Scorching overtook her completely. She rode him hard, taking her pleasure with every stroke and roll of her hips. The tempo quickened, then quickened again, their bodies coming together in a crescendo of wants and needs that neither of them could deny.

She reached the breaking point before him, giving him the chance to watch her come apart as she orgasmed. Every pulse of her inner walls pushed him closer to his own release, and as she cried out his name in rapture, his world exploded.

Belatedly, he remembered what would come next, and he pulled her into his arms as his cock thickened and swelled, locking them together as he emptied himself into her.

"What?" she gasped.

"It is our way." He whispered, then lost his voice as another wave of pleasure hit him. "Only with our mate can we find complete release." He finally managed to explain.

"Only with...you mean you've never?"

"Never. Like this." He thrust into her again. "Only with you."

Her lovely face lit up with a smile that filled his heart with a new kind of fire. A deep, warming flame that would never die.

"Joran!" Maggie's call tore him out of his fugue. She was still atop him, and her eyes glowed with emerald fire as she stared at him.

"Your eyes." They both spoke at the same time.

"Gold," she said.

"Glowing green," he replied. Understanding dawned a moment later. There had been no time to warn her about the changes he'd undergo when he claimed his mate. His eyes were gold now, a sign of his status, and confirmation that he had unlocked his ability to manipulate fire. He was a true Pyrosian. And so, it would appear, was his mate.

"Your eyes are like molten gold now. They were brown before, but they turned gold a few times, just for a second. Is this another thing you forgot to tell me?"

"I have a great deal of explaining to do, don't I?"

She flexed her inner walls around him. "You really do. And what do you mean, my eyes are glowing?"

"It would appear that undergoing the Scorching has awakened your Pyrosian genes. I'm not sure what else might have changed, but your eyes are now gleaming the most amazing shade of green. You are going to be the envy of every female on Pyros."

"Pyrosian genes? What?" She sat up and folded her arms across her chest. Looking every inch the queen she would one day be. "Start talking. Now."

Flames, she was glorious when she stood up to him. He was grinning as he reached up and set his hand on her arm. "We have a little time before the Scorching takes us again. I will tell you what I can before that happens."

"And how long does this Scorching thing last?"

"Approximately two of your solar cycles—days."

"Two days? Remind me later to let my friends know I'm not going to be around for a while."

"I will remind you, *seska*." And when he did, they would need to discuss what she would tell them when she left this world, and them, behind her forever. Her destiny lay elsewhere.

## 5

If the Scorching had lasted much longer, Maggie wasn't sure she would have survived it. Even after falling into a long, dreamless sleep on the second night, she still felt like she'd run back-to-back marathons. She had delicious aches in the most interesting places, which was why she was lingering in Joran's shower, letting the hot water work its magic while she tried to wrap her head around everything that had happened since meeting Joran.

She was mated to an alien. An alien *prince*. That much, she'd accepted. One look in the mirror had confirmed her eyes were a blazing emerald now, just as Joran's were now a gleaming gold. He'd gained access to his powers too. At least, that's what he'd told her. He could snap his fingers and summon a flame that danced on his outstretched palm without burning him. It didn't burn her either, a fact they'd discovered when he'd burst into flames during sex. She laughed as she recalled the look on his face.

Everything about their time together had been memorable, but now that her mind was clear again, she had questions and concerns that Joran didn't seem to be taking seriously. For him, it was obvious. She was his mate, and that meant she would be returning to Pyros with him. She had to make him see that for her, it wasn't so simple.

She had a life here. Friends she cared about. She wasn't going to abandon her entire world and follow him across the galaxy because of a damned spark and two days of lust-fueled fireworks. Granted, they'd been the best fireworks she'd ever experienced, but that wasn't enough to make her turn her back on her friends and her plans. Nice, safe plans for a small and simple life. There was nothing small or simple about moving to an alien world as the mate of a damned *prince*.

She returned to the main room of Joran's quarters and smiled when she saw that Joran had laid out her freshly cleaned clothes for her. Or maybe he'd had one of the service droids do it. He seemed to enjoy ordering the machines around, sending them to fetch everything they'd needed for the past few days. The droids, and the guards. God, she'd nearly died of embarrassment when she first realized they weren't alone on the ship. No matter how good the soundproofing was, they had to have heard enough to know exactly what she and Joran were up to.

Once she was dressed and she'd done what she could with her hair, she left his quarters and wandered the ship, looking for him. She hadn't been outside his room since they'd come on board, but something guided her through the ship, as if she could sense his presence, which didn't seem possible. But then again, impossible things had been happening with alarming frequency of late.

Her instincts led her to another door panel, and she waved her hand over it, unsure if it would open for her. It did, and the moment the wall vanished, she was hit with the enticing aroma of breakfast. A real, human breakfast, with eggs and bacon and buttered toast. Her stomach rumbled loudly, announcing her arrival even before she could say hello.

"I thought you'd enjoy something familiar to eat, so I sent my men to pick up a takeout order." Joran hesitated slightly over the slang phrase, but it was still amazing to her that he hadn't been able to speak any English at all less than a month ago. He crossed the room and offered her his hand, flashing her a pleased smile when she took it.

Instead of leading her to the table, he turned and faced the two men standing at the far end of what must be the dining area. A gleaming table was surrounded by comfortable looking chairs. The floor was the same soft-hued orange as the rest of the ship, but the pale-coloured walls were livened up by several large monitors displaying pictures of what must be Pyros. The sky was a paler shade of blue than Earth, and there were two moons in the sky in several of the pictures.

Joran spoke, and she turned her head to watch as he said something to the others in his own language, then spoke in English. "Guardsman Tarjen and Keth, this is my mate, Maggie O'Hara. Maggie, these are two of my most loyal guards. Now that we are mated, their duties include keeping you safe at all times."

Both men saluted, right arms crossing their chests, palms flat against their crisp black uniforms. "It is an honour to meet you, Highness," said the taller of the two. Both of them looked about the same age as Joran. They had dark hair and normal eyes, which she now knew meant that neither of them had found their mates, yet.

"Please, call me Maggie. I'm not going to know who you're talking to if you address me by Highness. That's him, not me." She tilted her head towards Joran.

The guards' eyes widened, and they both looked to Joran with confused expressions. Joran scowled at her. "You're my mate, which makes you their princess. The title is an expression of respect."

"Two days ago, I was a barista who didn't believe in aliens. Today, I'm mated to one. There are limits to how much I can adjust to, and I've pretty much reached them. There are a grand total of four people on this ship, so for now, can we please not worry about titles?"

"For now." Joran looked like he had more to say, but he was interrupted by the disembodied voice of the ship's computer. She had no idea what it said, but Joran reacted like he'd been hit with high voltage. He replied in his language and then turned to her. "My parents have made contact and wish to speak with me. Do you wish to be introduced now, or later when you've had more time to adjust?"

"Your parents? Please, not yet."

He flashed her a small, supportive smile that reminded her that he wasn't all bad. Arrogant, yes. Bossy, definitely. But he was also sweet and charming.

"I understand, and I'm sure they will, too. This has not been easy for you. I'll be back soon. Until then, enjoy breakfast." He was gone a moment later, leaving her alone with his guards. She corrected herself. *Their* guards.

She took her first real look at the food laid out on the table and laughed. Pancakes, waffles, bacon, sausages, eggs done several ways, and an entire platter of pastries was laid out, along with at least three different types of toast and disposable coffee cups that all had different notations on the side. "There's so much here, we'll be eating breakfast for the next three meals. So, what's been your favorite so far?"

"This repast is for you, High- Maggie. Keth and I will eat later."

"So, you're going to stand there and watch while I eat?" She shook her head. "I don't think so. Both of you, take a seat and help yourselves to anything you want while it's still warm."

Neither of them moved, and she decided it was time to test her new status. "C'mon, you two. Sit. Or am I going to have to make that a command?"

"It's not protocol." Tarjen protested, but she saw the way he was looking at the waffles and knew he was tempted.

"I'm betting it's not proper protocol for the Crown Prince to fly across the galaxy to abduct his mate, either."

Keth spluttered, and Tarjen actually grinned for a split second.

"That's what I thought." She took a seat at one end of the table and searched through the coffee cups until she found one marked as a simple latte. As soon as she took a drink, she started feeling better. This was something familiar. Her stomach growled again as the enticing scent of cinnamon wafted past her.

The two guards were finally seated, but neither of them had started filling their plates, yet. "If you don't know where to start, I recommend the coffee.

Joran seemed to like it. Oh, and if you like sweet things, try the pastries. If you prefer savory, go for the meat and eggs. And if you can't decide, try the waffles." She gestured to each item as she mentioned it, then pointed to a container full of cinnamon rolls. "I'm starting with one of those, if you would please pass them to me?"

Fifteen minutes later, they were laughing and talking between bites of breakfast. Once they had gotten used to the idea of eating with royalty, Tarjen and Keth turned out to be good company. Better yet, they had served in the military with Joran, and it hadn't taken much prompting for them to start sharing stories of their time together.

"You two really need to meet my friends. I think you'd get along great. Who knows, maybe they could wind up being your mates," she said around a mouthful of toast.

"As honoured as we would be to meet with your friends, we aren't permitted to take a mate from this planet."

"What do you mean, you're not permitted? Joran said there were several of your ships in orbit right now, each with males looking to acquire mates from different parts of Earth."

Tarjen nodded. "There are. But those males are of..." he paused as he considered the correct phrasing. "Better birth than we are."

An icy knot formed in the pit of her stomach.

"You mean they're only allowing the rich and powerful to claim Earth women? I still don't agree that any of you have the right to take us away from our homes. But it's even worse that you've come all this way, and they're not even letting you have a chance to find your mate. This is so screwed up."

"There's too much at risk. If the— oof." Keth's sentence ended in a hiss of breath as Tarjen elbowed him in the stomach.

"If what? What's a risk?" What else had Joran forgotten to mention?"

"You will have to ask your mate that question," Tarjen told her.

"Oh, believe me, I'm going to." She put down her fork and pushed her plate a few inches away. She wasn't hungry anymore. "Maybe by the time we come back for a visit, things will have changed, and I can introduce you to...shit." In all the chaos, she'd forgotten that Lisa had also gotten a match on the Star-Crossed Dating site.

"What concerns you?" Keth asked, his food forgotten as he reacted to her outburst.

"My friend, Lisa. She signed up for the same website I did, and she got a match. Does that mean she's been targeted, too?"

Keth glanced over at Tarjen, looking mildly alarmed. They spoke to each other in Pyrosian, but she managed to catch a single word she recognized. Vadir.

"That was his name. Do you know him?"

"You will have to ask—" Tarjen started to speak, but she cut him off by slamming her hands down on the table so hard the dishes rattled.

"Don't you dare tell me to ask my mate again. You're supposed to be loyal to me, right? So, talk." She folded her arms across her chest and tried to look commanding. "And that's an order."

"Vadir was brought to Earth on the same vessel as the prince. He was matched to a female in your city. Since only two females were matched from this location, it is very likely your friend is his mate," Keth said.

"I guess that's good news. We can travel together when we come home to visit."

Keth frowned. "At the risk of angering you again, Highness. I suggest you speak to the prince about your plans to return to your planet in the future."

"You have got to be kidding me. He can't expect me to leave everything behind and never come back." She held up her hand before either of them could comment. "I know what 'talk to your mate' means. It means I'm not going to like what I hear."

She rose from the table, her hands fisted at her sides to hide the fact they were shaking. She needed to get away from here, away from Joran and this ship and all the craziness. She was finally clear-headed again, and she had a lot to think about. "How do I leave this ship?"

The guards were already on their feet, but both of them froze at her question. "You wish to leave?" Tarjen asked.

"I do. I just need one of you to tell me the way to the exit."

Neither of them said a word, but Keth shook his head almost imperceptibly. "You need to stay here."

"So, you're going to make me order you to tell me how to get out of here?"

"Our duty is to keep you safe. That is the one and only time we can disobey your orders. Leaving this ship without the Prince or one of us with you is a risk we cannot allow you to take."

"Seriously?" She stared at them, her frustration making it difficult to come back with a wittier response. "I live here! I wander through this city every day, all by myself, and survive just fine. I'll find a cab or a bus and make my way home."

"Maggie, we're not in the city anymore." Keth said a few words in Pyrosian, and the monitors all changed. The views of Pyros were gone, replaced with the deep greens and dappled shadows of the forest.

"You moved the ship." She didn't bother making it a question. Joran had said the teleportation device only worked for short range, and there was nothing like this primordial forest that close to Vancouver.

"Once we were back aboard, yes. It's easier to keep the ship undetected away from urban centres."

She was trapped on board this damned ship. Yet another thing Joran had forgotten to mention. She gave her guards a tight-lipped smile and tried not to let her frustration show. None of this was their fault. "Thank you for explaining. Since I can't go anywhere, else, I'll be in Joran's quarters. Please tell him to come find me when he's finished speaking to his parents."

"We'll relay your message," Tarjen said.

"Turn right and then go straight until you pass the fourth door. Your quarters are the next door on your left," Keth added.

"Thank you." She headed back the way she came with a head full of questions and a heart that weighed heavy in her chest. How much was she willing to sacrifice to make things work with a man she barely knew? More importantly, was Joran willing to sacrifice anything at all? If not, then this was never going to work.

***

Joran had ended his conversation with his parents on a high note. They had been elated to hear that he was mated, and could not wait to meet Maggie and welcome her into their family. His good mood had lasted until he'd returned to the dining area and heard from Keth and Tarjen.

Now, he was standing outside the door to his

own quarters, bracing himself for the firestorm waiting for him within.

"I know you're out there, so you might as well come in," Maggie called out in flat tones.

He should have known she could sense him. The bond between them was strengthening by the hour. They would never be alone again because they would always be able to sense the other's presence. The bond was different for each couple. Some mates could barely sense each other, while others could feel their partner's emotional state from a great distance. Only time would reveal how strong their link was.

He opened the door and stepped inside. "Maggie, I've been informed you are upset, and that you have more questions for me. Whatever you want to know, I'll explain as best I can."

His lovely mate was sitting on the corner of the bed, arms wrapped around herself and her head bowed.

"Is this how it's going to be, Joran? Is this what it means to be your mate?" She lifted her head, and his heart lurched when he saw the tears on her cheeks.

"I don't know what you mean, *seska*. This is new for both of us."

"That's just it. I don't think this is all that new for you." She gestured around her. "This is your ship. You're here with your men. You expect me to give up everything to follow you to *your* planet. What's changed for you?"

"What's changed for me? Everything!" I didn't think I had a mate. I'd come to accept that I was going to be the last of my line. That I would never rule. That's all changed now. Everything will be different when I get back, and while I am grateful to the Gods for gifting me with a mate, I'm not sure I'm ready to deal with the rest of it. This isn't easy for me, either, Maggie."

"You don't want to be king someday? I thought that's what this whole thing was about? Why else did your people only send the rich and powerful to claim mates? If this wasn't about you, then why aren't Keth and Tarjen even in your precious database of potential matches? They came all this way, and they don't even have a chance of being matched."

"They weren't supposed to mention that to you. It was something I wanted to discuss with you on our way back to Pyros."

"What if I don't want to go back with you?"

Her words sliced through him like an assassin's blade. "We're mated. I know you can feel the bond between us. That's never going to fade, Maggie. We're linked for life."

"But no one ever asked me if this is what I wanted. You talk about the Gods, and fate, and mating bonds, but you keep forgetting that none of that means anything to me."

"Sacrifice is our birthright." It was one of the first lessons his father had ever taught him, and now he needed to explain it to his mate. "I was born to rule Pyros, and you were destined to rule at my side. This is what must happen, Maggie. It's the will of the Gods."

She sliced through the air with the edge of her hand. "Enough. It might be their will, but it's not mine. Take me home, Joran. I'd have left already, but apparently, we're in the middle of a damned forest, and your men won't let me outside for fear that their future queen will be devoured by the local wildlife."

"I'll have them fly us closer to your home, and we can teleport back."

"Or you can set me down somewhere, and I'll call a cab. Once we're close enough to civilization, I can call my friends. I haven't spoken to them since I left messages letting them know I was fine and spending some time with you. They have to be out of their minds with worry. At least, Gwen will be. Since Lisa was matched with your traveling buddy, Vadir, I can only assume she's deep in the thrall of the Scorching by now."

"Did you say your friend was matched to Vadir?" He ran a hand through his hair in frustration. He'd only left for a short time. How had everything fallen apart so flaming fast? And how had the link between

Maggie and Lisa been missed? This mission was getting messier by the moment.

"Yes, my friend Lisa signed up for the same site I did. In fact, she's the one who talked both Gwen and I into doing it at all. With everything that happened, I forgot about her, which is something I'm not proud of. I need to find out if she's okay. Please? Let me go, Joran."

"I will accompany you home. There is still much we need to discuss."

"Just once, do you think you could try asking me what I want instead of telling me what's going to happen next?"

He started to argue but cut himself off before he added more fuel to the fire of her temper. "I will leave you alone while I arrange for our return."

He paused and softened his tone before asking, "Would you like the guards to accompany us as well, or would you prefer it if I went with you alone?"

"I'd prefer it if I was going home by myself, but since that doesn't seem to be an option, I'd rather not drag the others along. I already owe them both an apology for my temper."

"You do not need to apologize—"

"Oh yes, I do. And if you think that being royalty means never having to acknowledge your mistakes, then that explains a whole hell of a lot. Please let me know when it's time to go."

He ached to go to her, wrap her in his arms and

kiss her until she had forgotten her upset, but something told him that wouldn't work. As he left, it occurred to him that she had dismissed him with the regality of a born queen. He accepted that the Gods had chosen the perfect female for him. Now, he needed to somehow convince Maggie that her destiny wasn't to stay on Earth, but to accompany him to Pyros and rule at his side.

**6**

———

It didn't take long for Keth to pilot the ship back within teleportation range of Maggie's home. It took a little more time for Joran to convince his guards to stay behind. Keth and Tarjen were still irked with him for ditching them the last time he'd left the ship. In the end, they only agreed to it because Maggie preferred to return home alone. They might not have known her very long, but she had apparently made an impression.

He knew exactly how they felt.

Maggie didn't say anything when he returned to his quarters to tell her they had arrived. She rose from the bed and joined him in the corridor with nothing more than a slight nod to indicate she was ready to go. Her expression was guarded, and her movements were slow and listless. As if the fire in her soul had been snuffed out.

When they got to the airlock, he held out his hand, but she didn't move to take it.

"We'll need to be in contact when we teleport," he reminded her.

"We have to do that again? Can't we just leave the ship?" She gestured to the barren space of the airlock. "Why do we have to come into the airlock to teleport, anyway?"

"The device on my wrist is only one small part of the equipment required to make even a short jump. The rest of it is set up inside the walls of this room. It acts as an amplifier of sorts. The airlock is the safest place to transfer in and out of because it's completely empty. That ensures there's nothing present that we could uh, get tangled up with."

Maggie went pale. "You mean if we materialized into the same space as something else, we could end up merged with whatever it was on a molecular level? And you still use this insane method of transport?"

"There are many safeguards in place to make sure that does not happen. It does limit where we can materialize, however. It has to be somewhere clear of debris, and out of sight. Which is why we're not going to walk off this ship. We're cloaked right now, but if someone saw two people suddenly materialize out of thin air, there would be questions."

"I think you're underestimating humanity's ability to willfully ignore anything they don't want to know about, but I concede your point." She sighed and took his hand. "Is this going to suck as much as it did last time?"

"This time, you'll know what's happening. We'll appear less than a block from your home. It's a safe landing site, I promise."

She furrowed her brows and tightened her grip on his hand. "If I end up merged with a tree or something, I'm going to be really pissed at you."

"I would never let anything happen to you, Maggie. Whatever else you might think of me, you can trust in that."

He threaded his fingers through hers and then lifted both their hands to activate the device on his wrist. He braced himself for the mind-shredding sonic assault that heralded the beginning of their journey, followed by the stomach-twisting transition into the void. No matter how many times he endured it, he would never get used to the soul-crushing emptiness.

This time, the journey was different. He wasn't alone. He could sense Maggie through their bond. In the eternal darkness of this place, she was a beacon of light and life. He focused on that, on *her*, and the loneliness faded. In this space between spaces, there could be no words. They had no bodies to touch with, no senses to distract them. There were only the two of them, reaching for each other across the infinite void.

In that moment, he could feel what she felt. There was grief, resentment, and confusion, but there was something else mixed in with her pain. There was hope.

When he returned to the world, the connection grew weaker, but he knew what he'd felt. Senses scrambled, eyes still closed, he instinctively drew her into his arms. She leaned into him, her head on his chest and her body trembling as he held her.

"I felt you," she whispered, her voice tinged with awe.

"I could feel you, too. The bond between us is strong." He bowed his head to brush a kiss to the crown of her hair, buying himself a few more seconds before he offered her the choice she'd been denied until now.

"I think it's strong enough to let us stay in contact no matter how far apart we are. Even if there was a galaxy between us."

"A galaxy? You mean...?"

The thought of leaving his *seska* behind made his heart ache, but she was right. She hadn't been given a choice in anything that had happened since the moment they'd met. He kept promising to make things up to her, but how could he make amends for ripping her out of her life here on Earth? She deserved to have a say in her future, even if it cost him dearly. "If you wish to stay here, Maggie, then I will respect your choice. I want you with me, but not at the cost of your happiness."

"Thank you." Tipping her head up to look at him for the first time, she smiled. "I don't know what I wish. Not yet. I need to understand all of this better. And I need to talk to my friends. Please? I know this is supposed to be a secret, but Lisa knows about Vadir by now, and Gwen... Shit. Lisa and I were the only ones matched from this city. Gwen wasn't. I can't leave her here alone. She's like a sister to me."

"Let's go inside." He brushed his fingers over her soft cheek and wondered where he'd find the strength to leave her if she decided to stay.

She looked around, her eyes widening as she recognized where they were standing. "I'm almost home. It just occurred to me that means you knew where I lived when we first met and you asked if you could escort me home. You knew where I worked, too, didn't you? You lied to me from the moment we met."

"I wasn't supposed to be there at all," he confessed as he finally let her go.

"You weren't?"

"You can ask Keth and Tarjen about it sometime. I ditched them and came to the coffee shop to see you. I was supposed to wait until we made contact on the site. I couldn't wait. Everything that happened after that was my fault. The Spark, the Scorching, taking you to my ship before you knew what was going on, none of that was part of the plan. I put you through so much. I am sorry, Maggie."

She took a step, then reached back to take his hand. It was a small gesture, but as far as he was concerned, it was a major victory.

"I know you're sorry. That's a good start, but you still lied to me, Joran. If we have any chance of making this work, that has to stop."

"After what we experienced in the void, I don't think we can lie to each other anymore. Our link is too strong. You'd know if I was keeping something from you."

Her fingers tightened around his. "Then this is going to be a fascinating conversation. You can start by telling me how you ended up in my coffee shop ahead of schedule, and then we're going to talk about why only the rich and powerful men of your planet are being sent to find mates."

"This is going to be a long conversation."

"I'll make coffee." She started walking. "And if there's no such thing as coffee on your planet, then you better figure out a way to import it if you want me to live there. Coffee is life."

"If that's what it takes to convince you to come back to Pyros with me, I'll find a way." Flames, he'd rearrange the stars to spell out her name if he thought it would help. He needed her at his side, challenging him, pushing him to be better. When his parents had told him about this plan, he'd been more concerned about how it would affect his people, and himself. He'd simply assumed he would be able to convince Maggie and the others to come to Pyros because that was what was needed.

When Maggie had pointed that out, Joran responded the same way his father had done. He was ashamed to realize that after all his protests against taking a mate against her will, that was what he'd been trying to do. The Scorching had clouded his thinking, but that was no excuse for what he'd said and done. It had to be her choice.

To save his people, they needed human females. To ensure that happened, he needed Maggie. She held the fate of his people in one hand and his heart in the other.

***

Maggie couldn't hang onto her anger anymore. Not after what she'd experienced in the void. The first time she'd gone through that ordeal, it had terrified her. The infinite expanse of silent nothingness was the stuff of nightmares. It reminded her of the long, lonely nights she'd spent in foster care feeling lost and invisible. This time, everything was different. She hadn't been alone. She didn't understand how the link worked, but somehow, Joran had been with her in the darkness.

How many times as a girl had she prayed for

someone to ease her loneliness? How many tear-soaked wishes had she made over the years? He'd been there for her, offering her comfort even as he'd given her a glimpse into who he really was. There was pride, but also worry and regret. There was courage, too, and determination, but the strongest of all, was the love in his heart. Love for his home. For his people. His family...and for her.

After experiencing all of that, she'd have to be a fool to turn her back and let him leave without her. He was the embodiment of every wish she'd ever made. The universe, or maybe Joran's Gods, had actually sent her a handsome prince straight out of a fairy tale. Life with him wouldn't be perfect, but it would be more of a life than she was living now.

"Fortune favors the bold," she muttered, recalling one of her father's favorite sayings.

"What was that?" Joran asked.

"I was remembering something my dad used to say. I haven't thought about him in a long time."

She glanced back at Joran as they crossed the street and headed towards her front door. "I think he would have liked you. He liked to push his luck, too."

He grinned at her, and his golden eyes gleamed in the sunlight. "If that phrase means what I think it does, then I suspect I would have liked your father, too. My people are known for testing limits and challenging Fate itself. It is a trait we value, and one that my family is known for. My mother tempers that quality in my father. If I am truly blessed, I hope you'll be able to do the same for me."

"You mean, like stopping you from charging into a coffee shop and initiating the Scorching with a woman you've never met?"

"Exactly like that." He tugged on her hand, drawing her close enough that he could slant a brief but sizzling kiss across her lips.

Joy and lust zinged through her veins in a heady cocktail that made her head spin and her heart pound. She wasn't ready to say yes, yet. There were things she still needed to know, and friends she had to talk to.

"Let's get inside before someone stops looking at your hot body long enough to notice your eyes are an impossible shade of gold."

He reached out to gently tap his forefinger beside her right eye. "If you stay here, you're going to have to hide those beautiful eyes of yours, too. Or had you forgotten that the Scorching changed us both?"

Her hand flew up to touch his. "Damn it! I did forget. So much for playing it cool with Gwen. She's going to notice the difference right away." She took a deep breath and headed up the stairs with Joran falling in behind her.

Once she was inside, she called out for Gwen and Lisa, though she didn't expect Lisa to be back yet. It was Gwen's day off, though, which meant she should be home.

No one answered her greeting. She even knocked on Gwen's door, but there was no response.

"I'll call Gwen and let her know I'm alright. She's probably worried sick by now, and there wasn't any cell service in the middle of the forest." A thought occurred, and she flicked Joran an annoyed glance. "Was that part of the reason you moved the ship so far away?"

"No. Tarjen and Keth insisted we move to make it easier to avoid detection. Actually, that was the first thing that went according to plan. I didn't even remember they were going to do it until I walked into the cockpit of the ship to talk to my parents this morning and noticed the change in scenery."

"I guess we were both a little distracted. One sec, let me make this call."

She pulled out her phone and groaned. The last time she'd looked, there had still been a little juice left, but after two days without recharging, the battery had finally died. "Good thing we have a land-line." She jogged down the hall a little way to where an old fashioned, wall-mounted phone sat. She'd never used it, but Gwen insisted on paying for a line in case they ever needed it.

There was no answer on Gwen or Lisa's cell phones. It went straight through to voicemail for them both so she left messages and tried not to worry. Much.

"Come on. My place is this way." She led Joran to

her suite downstairs. Lisa had the attic since it had the best light for her painting, and they had given Gwen the main floor because it was the one with the biggest kitchen, and Gwen loved to cook.

"Remember when I called your quarters opulent?" She asked as she unlocked the door and stepped inside. "This is what I was comparing it to."

Lisa often joked that Maggie must have been a troll in a previous life, which was why she didn't mind living in a cave. Caves didn't have windows, though, and Maggie's suite did have one. Granted, it was only two feet high, had a view of the weeds that choked the flower bed outside, and was partially obscured by the heavy steel security bars, but it was still a window.

He followed her inside, and she felt a pang of embarrassment. She'd worked hard to buy what little she had, but seeing it now, it all looked shabby and plain. Her few furnishings were mismatched and threadbare, the carpet was worn, and the only thing of any real value was a painting of a gull soaring over an expanse of sunlit ocean. Lisa had painted it and given it to her for her thirtieth birthday. She said it was to make sure that there was always a bit of sunshine in Maggie's life.

"Not everyone lives like I do. I'm not going to judge your worth based on the value of the things you own. We're far from a perfect species, but we have learned at least that much." He grinned. "There are members of the Inter-Planetary Council who would say that's all we've learned."

"You can add that to the list of things I need to learn about." She plugged in her phone, settled onto the couch, and gestured for Joran to join her.

He sat down next to her and took her hand in his. "I think I should start at the beginning. There's so much I need to explain. Things you should have been told before we got this far."

"So you've mentioned." She squeezed his hand. "Tell me."

## 7

It was more than an hour later before she finally felt like she had a basic understanding of everything Joran was telling her.

"So, you're telling me that your people acquired black market tech to go on a quest to find females before your species faces extinction? And this council of worlds or whatever they're called doesn't know that you're here, on Earth, because you're not supposed to approach any species until they reach some arbitrary list of developmental milestones."

His lips twitched. "Your assessment is remarkably similar to what I said when my parents first informed me of their plan."

"And what did they say to you?"

"Father gave me his duty, honour, and sacrifice speech, while mother claimed it was the will of the Gods."

She blinked. "Wait, weren't those the lines you gave me just this morning?"

Joran bowed his head, and she watched as a faint blush stained his cheeks right up to the tips of his ears. "It was."

"I think your Gods are out of their minds. Out of an entire universe, they picked me to be your mate. What do I know about being a princess? Or a queen for that matter? I serve overpriced coffee to strangers for a living. They should have chosen someone else."

"I don't want someone else." He lifted his head to stare at her with his incredible golden eyes. "The only woman I want, is you."

She felt the truth of his words resonate through the bond they shared. Powerful. Undeniable. He meant every word, and her heart sang with hope. This was everything she'd dreamed of, but it was also more. So much more. To be with Joran, she'd have to forsake her plans to live small and simple. If she said yes, then everything changed.

Joran took her hand and gripped it tightly. "You're still having doubts."

"Wouldn't you?"

He gave her a tender smile. "We're bound together, Maggie. You know the truth of what I'm saying. Trust me. Please."

She focused on the link between them. She couldn't sense his thoughts directly, but she could feel his emotions. He cared about her. Deeply. He was worried, too. Worried she would say no. That he'd spend the rest of his life without her, alone.

She knew that fear intimately. She'd carried it with her since her father's death. At that moment, she made her decision. This was her chance, and if she didn't take it, she'd likely never have the courage to try again. She wasn't going to let her fear hold her back. Not this time. "You're sure?" she asked.

"I have never been more certain of anything in my life."

"Then I guess we're going to find out if your Gods know what they're doing."

He started to speak, but she raised a finger before he could say a word. "If you promise me that Lisa and Gwen can come, too. Mated or not. I'm not leaving them behind unless they chose to stay."

A powerful sense of determination flowed through their link, and she knew without a doubt that he'd find a way to bring her friends to Pyros for her.

"If they want to leave, then I'll make sure your friends accompany us back to Pyros. You have my word, *seska*." He barely finished speaking before he had her in his lap, his strong arms wrapped around her as he crushed his mouth to hers.

His hands framed her face, tipping her head up as he kissed her with a ferocity that took her breath away. She moaned and he pressed in closer, his tongue delving into her mouth to tangle with hers as his hands left her face to take hold of her hips. Without breaking their kiss, he lifted her, turning her so she was straddling his thighs, the hard length of his cock pressed against her core.

Need coursed like molten metal through her veins, and she reacted out of instinct, grinding herself against him as she twined her arms around his neck. Joran's hands slid up from her hips, spanning her rib cage and then sweeping up to cup her breasts in his hands. Every touch made the fire inside her burn hotter. Her clit throbbed in time to her pounding heart, and every part of her was aching with need.

Joran lifted his head and she gasped for breath, filling her lungs with cool air that did nothing to ease the heat sizzling through her.

"Tell me you're mine," he whispered, staring into her eyes.

"I'm yours. I will be your Queen, your mate, your everything." She recalled the words he'd spoken to her the first time they'd been together. "And you will be mine from now until we return to the Flame."

The smile he gave her was brighter than a thousand suns. "You remembered."

"Did I say it right?"

"You said it perfectly, my mate."

Pure joy surged through her, and she belatedly realized that Joran was the source.

"Why are you so happy?"

"Because I have you. I need you, Maggie. Not as my queen, or to hold onto the throne, or as the future mother of my children." He laid his hand over her heart, then over his. "I didn't know how empty my life was until I found you."

She laid her hand over his and opened her heart to him. "I stopped believing in fairy tales and magic a long time ago. I thought it was easier to live that way. Then you came along and showed me that there is still magic in the universe. How else could you have found me?"

Her words were still hanging in the air between them as he kissed her again, this time with a tender passion that erased everything but the heat of his touch and the waves of need that pounded her relentlessly.

For the second time in as many days, he stripped her out of the same top, only this time he tore it off and let the tattered scraps fall to the floor. He kissed his way down her body, leaving a trail of fire from her lips to her throat to the rise of her breasts. When his lips brushed over her diamond-hard nipple, she gasped and arched her back in silent offering. He sucked her nipple into his mouth, lashing at it with his tongue until she was squirming in his lap.

By the time he raised his head again, his eyes

were glowing a brilliant gold. Without a word, he helped her stand, then rose from the couch to help her out of the rest of her clothes.

"My bed is in there," she pointed through the archway that led to her tiny room and even smaller bed. It was twin sized, and she had no idea how Joran would ever fit on it.

"We can stay right here," he said after a quick glance. "More space."

He pulled his shirt over his head, and all the air in the room vanished. It might have only been a few hours since she'd seen him naked, but somehow she didn't think she'd ever get used to the sight. Unable to resist, she brushed her fingers down the sculpted lines of his stomach, tracing a path down until her fingers were stroking over the hard ridge of his cock.

"Keep going. I like having your hands on me." The hunger in his voice amplified her own needs and she undid his pants with trembling fingers. Just like before, he wasn't wearing underwear. His thick length fell into her hand, and she wrapped her fingers around him, stroking him with strong, slow pulls the way she'd learned he liked it best.

"Flames, the things you make me feel."

He stripped off the rest of his clothes so quickly he almost lost his balance getting one sock off, and somehow that led to them landing in a breathless, laughing tangle on the floor of her living room.

They were still laughing when he moved over

her, nudging her legs apart as he settled his big body into the cradle of her thighs. "I need you," he murmured, leaning down to kiss her.

"I need you, too." She stroked her fingers through his hair and then wrapped one leg around his hips, pulling him in tight.

---

Joran knew the Scorching was over, but his need for Maggie hadn't waned at all. If anything, it was stronger and more focused. His hunger for her ran soul-deep. Looking down at his mate, he felt as if he was looking at a banquet that he could feast on for the rest of his life.

"Mine, forever." He let his cock slide into her slick folds, priming her body with slow, teasing strokes. He didn't take it further until she was trembling beneath him and her breathy moans took on an urgent edge. That was when he claimed her in one, slow-and-steady thrust that didn't end until he was completely sheathed inside her.

The walls of her pussy flexed around his cock, and he let himself go. She met him thrust for thrust, their passion growing and merging until they were both out of control.

Nails scored his back, the biting sting only adding more fuel to the inferno raging inside him. He tried to slow his pace, but she wouldn't let him.

instead, she made love to him with her mouth, her tongue dancing with his, echoing the joining of their bodies.

He pounded into her, groaning her name as his orgasm built to a crescendo. She came with a wild cry, her body tightening around him as his cock thickened and swelled and his world went up in flames. He was a slave to the sensations coursing through him as he came, and it wasn't until his senses finally calmed that he heard Maggie giggling.

"Well, there goes my damage deposit."

"Huh?" The carpet around her was blackened and scorched. "Oops."

"You can say that again. Is this going to happen often? If so, we're going to need fireproof sheets."

"I'll learn to control it, in time." He leaned in to kiss her. "Until then, best we avoid making love anywhere with flammable materials. I should have remembered the risk. I am sorry about the damage."

"It's not like I'm going to need my damage deposit, anyway. I'm not going to live here much longer, right? Shit, I have a lot to organize before then. I'm going to be busy."

"We'll leave for the *Firebrand* in a few cycles. After that, we'll break orbit and begin the journey home. It will take some time to put enough distance between Earth and us that we can use the rift generator without being detected."

"And how long until we reach your planet? Weeks? Months?"

"Less than an Earth week. The journey through the rift only takes a few minutes. We'll make the rest of the journey in the normal way, and it will appear as if we never left the system."

"Days, huh? Then we better make the most of our honeymoon. It's going to be a short one."

He rocked his hips, gently pumping his still engorged cock deeper into her body. "We have the rest of our lives together, *seska*. And I intend to make love to you every day we are given."

She smiled up at him. "I like that plan. I've only got one more question before we put it into action. What does *seska* mean? You still haven't told me."

"It means beloved of my heart. And that's what you are to me, Maggie O'Hara. You are my beloved. The one destined to claim my heart."

She was laughing as she lifted her head to kiss him. "I promise to take good care of it, Joran Pyr. From now until the Flames claim us both.

They talked some more, and then made love in the shower where there was no risk of Joran setting the house on fire. By the time she was dressed and feeling like herself again, she still hadn't heard from either Gwen or Lisa. The silence was worrying.

"I should have heard back by now. Is there any way you can contact Vadir and at least confirm that Lisa is with him?"

Joran nodded. "I'll have Kash ping his ship's computer. Even if Vadir's still in the thrall of the Scorching, the ship should be able to tell us if he's aboard, and who might be with him."

"The computer? What about his guards?"

"No guards. Vadir likes to do things for himself. He's stubborn about things like that. He even pilots his own ship. Why don't you try calling your friends again, and I'll contact Kash."

She called Lisa's number first. It went straight to voicemail again. Gwen's rang through, but there was no answer. Where were her friends and why weren't they answering their phones?

Joran was still speaking in Pyrosian by the time she finished the second call. She had no idea what he was saying, but when he started to smile, she felt a pang of hope that he'd had better luck than she had.

The moment he stopped talking, he tucked the device back into his pocket and grinned at her. "You can stop worrying. Your friends are fine. Both of them."

She jumped to her feet. "Where? How? Are they okay? Why aren't they answering their phones?"

"They're both fine. The rest of your questions you can ask them yourself. I've got their coordinates.

We'll hop back to the ship, and I'll have Keth fly us there."

"Let's go!" She bounced over to his side and took his hand. "Poof us back to the ship already."

"I will, but not yet. Your friends have a request for you. They'd like you to bring them some clothes."

"Clothes? Why would--Oh. Oh my. Both of them?"

"Both. It would seem the Gods have been busy."

She burst out laughing. "It would seem so. Oh, this is such good news!"

She packed quickly, handing items to Joran as she raced from room to room. Cosmetics, clothes, hair brush, shoes. More or less everything she'd wished she had when she woke up on Joran's ship this morning. When the bag was full, a wicked thought occurred to her and she darted back into Gwen's place for one last item.

"What is *that*?" Joran asked as she reappeared, staring at the bright red canister she'd liberated from under Gwen's sink.

"A fire extinguisher. We should probably invest in a few more before we leave."

He wrapped an arm around her waist and pulled her in for a heated kiss. "We'll add it to the list. Hang on to me, I'm taking us back to the ship, now."

She hung on tight and closed her eyes as the ear-piercing shriek heralded the start of another teleportation. This time, though, she didn't dread the journey through the void. Joran was with her, and that made all the difference.

With her mate at her side and her friends at her back, she was ready for whatever the Gods had planned. *Let the adventure begin.*

*The End*

VADIR
Star-crossed Alien Mail Order Brides #2

*What do you do when your planet runs out of women?
Send for takeout, of course.*

Vadir has a business empire to run and no time to spare on frivolous endeavors. So how did he wind up on the far side of the galaxy to claim a mate he never signed up for? A matchmaking queen and a royal decree, that's how.

His plan is simple: meet the female, negotiate terms, and leave the primitive planet of Earth as fast as he can. What could possibly go wrong?

This book contains a bohemian blonde with a hell of a right hook, and an interstellar tycoon who is about to learn that the best things in life can't be bought or sold, they have to be won.

**Keep Reading for a peek at Vadir and Lisa's story.**

Vadir Rahal paced the floor of his office and tried to think of a way out of this insane predicament. He didn't have time for this right now. What was the King thinking?

Turning his back on the sweeping view of the city outside his windows, he stormed back to his desk and snatched the thick piece of parchment off the surface. No one used parchment anymore. It had been an outdated concept two hundred years ago, but the royal family loved their traditions. The damned thing had even been delivered by a royal messenger in full uniform. He read the words again, looking for a loophole. Something, anything that he could use to decline the *honour* bestowed on him by the King and Queen of Pyros. There wasn't one.

"By the Flames of the First One, why did it had

to be me?" he tossed the royal decree back onto the desktop and started pacing again.

"I've got a half-dozen deals to broker in the next ten days, and the Qualla Mining Consortium is threatening a work stoppage that could affect the ore markets for years to come. I need to be here, not on the other side of the galaxy retrieving my mate. I don't need a mate. I didn't ask for one. Crown Prince Joran is the one who needs a..."

He stopped in his tracks. Joran. If anyone could get him out of this, it would be him. He activated a wall monitor and called the one man on the planet who had any chance of changing the King's mind.

"So, I guess you got the decree?" Joran asked by way of greeting.

"You knew about this?"

The Prince nodded. "I'm going with you. Turns out, you're not the only one whose mate is supposedly on that planet."

"Why me? Is this because I refused to play nice with the Romak during that last trade war? Is this your father's idea of revenge?"

"Wrong parent."

"Your *mother* did this to me? I thought she liked me!"

"She does. Which is why she insisted your profile be included when we screened for possible mates. The rest was luck, or if you believe my mother, the will of the Gods."

"So, this is real? My mate is out there?" The air in his perfectly maintained office suddenly seemed too thin.

"That's what the experts say. They may not be our true mates, but our scientists confirm we can have children with them."

"How can they possibly know that?"

Joran laughed. "I asked the same question. The answer is hard to believe, but I've seen the verified reports. Some of these people, humans, already carry Pyrosian genes."

"How?" Vadir demanded, too stunned by the revelation to manage more than a single word.

"I'll send you the report, and our experts' best guess as to how it happened. It makes for interesting reading, but the short version is, this is real."

"Our mates are out there, on another planet? And we're just going to wander over there, explain matters, and bring them back here? Do you know how insane that sounds?"

Joran nodded. "I know. Read the reports. Make whatever preparations you have to, and tell no one where you're going. The *Firebrand* leaves in twelve solar cycles. We've both been commanded to be on board. I don't recommend being late."

"I wouldn't dream of it. An order is an order." And apparently this was one command he wasn't going to be able to charm or buy his way around. Vadir recalled the final line of the missive he'd received. *You will go to Earth and determine if the female is your mate. If she is, then you are hereby commanded to bring her home to Pyros.*

"There's more at stake than you know. This is one command no one is going to be allowed to decline."

"Then I'll see you in twelve cycles. I don't suppose I'm going to be allowed to do some trade negotiations while I'm there?"

Joran laughed at him. "Father said you'd ask, and his answer is no."

"I had to ask."

"Of course you did. We'll talk again soon. I'll send you over the file with all the information we have on your match. It's not much, but at least you can see what she looks like. Her name is Lisa."

"Thanks."

Joran signed off, leaving Vadir alone in his office.

*I'm going to be mated.* The thought hit him with the force of a rogue comet strike. He'd never imagined this day would come. Hadn't planned for it. Why would he when there were so few unmated females on Pyros? He enjoyed the occasional dalliance with females from the planets he visited for business, but those were simple, short-term affairs. Taking a mate was anything but simple, which was why Vadir had hoped to avoid it. But not even his wealth and power allowed him to refuse a royal command.

Faced with a new challenge, Vadir did what he did best. He set aside his emotions and focused on making a plan. He'd just been ordered negotiate the biggest deal of his life, and failure was not an option. If the King and Queen wished him to bring back a mate, then that's what he'd do.

He returned to his desk and located the file Joran had mentioned. He needed to know as much about this Lisa as he could. Every being he'd ever met had a price. This female would be no exception. All he had to do was determine what she wanted, and offer it to her in exchange for leaving her primitive, isolated world to join him on Pyros and live in luxury for the rest of her life. It should be an easy sell.

Business had been slow all day, but that suited Lisa Woods just fine. She was still nursing a hangover from the wine she'd drunk last night. Or maybe it was an ice cream overdose. She pondered that idea for a moment and then rejected it. There was no such thing as too much ice cream.

There had definitely been too much wine, though. That's the only reason she had broken her vow to never go back to online dating. Apparently, four glasses was all it took to drown out the voice of reason. The proof was in her email inbox this morning: confirmation of registration to the Star-Crossed Dating Service.

At least she hadn't done it alone. She'd dragged Maggie and Gwen along with her on a quest for what the email promised would be an out of this world dating experience.

"I could use a little out of this world," she mused to herself as she looked around. Vancouver was a beautiful city, but it was easy to forget that when you never got to compare it to anywhere else. Lisa had spent her whole life here, and she dreamed of taking off to explore the world someday. Someday was still a long way off, though, considering she barely earned enough money to eat and make her rent.

Lisa made her living drawing caricatures and quick sketches for tourists. It wasn't exactly a glamorous or high-paying job, especially when the tourists were few and far between. It was still early in the season, which meant the artists and street performers that dotted the seawall outnumbered their potential customers. She could head home to work on her paintings, but the spring sunshine was too nice to head indoors yet.

She sat underneath the canopy of her umbrella, idly sketching her surroundings when inspiration struck. She opened her sketch book to a fresh page and started drawing, the world around her fading away as she worked. Apart from the occasional pause to push her blonde hair back from her face, she stayed focused on the face taking shape on the paper.

Her mystery man had dark hair with a hint of curl in it, a strong jaw, and a mouth that curved up into an arrogant smile. Try as she might, she couldn't get his eyes right, though. She'd drawn them dark and brooding, staring back at her from beneath a lightly furrowed brow. She kept working at them, and then, in a flash of insight, she knew what was wrong. She reached out with a bare foot to snag the strap of her crocheted art supply bag and pulled it close enough she could reach it without setting down the sketch book.

She fished out two of the the artist's pens she used for signing her work and considered them for a moment. Gold or silver? She dropped the silver one back into her bag and quickly added a few gold highlights to her creation's eyes.

"Better." She stared at the face she'd drawn, wondering where her muse had drawn her inspiration from this time. It wasn't a face she recognized from television or the movies. And if she'd ever laid eyes on a man that good-looking in person, she'd damned sure wouldn't forget it. Especially not with those amazing eyes.

A breeze stirred, lifting her hair off her shoulders and ruffling the page of her book so that his eyes seemed to sparkle with silent amusement.

Lisa had long ago learned that when her muse

took over like this, it was because the universe was trying to tell her something. Her friends teased her about her it, but they knew it was true. After all, she'd drawn pictures of both Gwen and Maggie days before they'd met. She'd drawn other things, too. Warnings that she had been too young and innocent to understand at the time. She wasn't innocent anymore, though. These days, when the universe whispered in her ear, she listened.

The wind came up again, lifting the hem of her skirt so that it swirled around her legs and sending goose bumps chasing down her spine. Something was coming. She stared down at the picture in her hands. Or *someone*.

KASH

Star-crossed Alien Mail Order Brides #3

*What do you do when your planet runs out of women? Send for takeout, of course.*

Kash knows he'll never be allowed to claim a mate. A lifetime of military service has left him too battle-scarred and broken to be considered for the off-world mating project his rulers have created to save their people.

His job is to make sure the more fortunate males get to Earth to retrieve their mates. All he has to do is pilot the ship, stay undetected, and keep an eye on things from orbit. It should be the easiest mission of his career...until he lays eyes on the one thing he never expected to find. His mate.

This book contains a hopeful romantic who is giving up hope, and a soldier who is about to discover that love doesn't obey orders, and it can't be bound by rules.

## ABOUT THE AUTHOR

Susan lives out on the Canadian west coast surrounded by open water, dear family, and good friends. She's jumped out of perfectly good airplanes on purpose and accidentally swum with sharks on the Great Barrier Reef.

If the world ends, she plans to survive as the spunky, comedic sidekick to the heroes of the new world, because she's too damned short and out of shape to make it on her own for long.

*You can find out more about Susan and her books here:*

www.susanhayes.ca
susan@susanhayes.ca

# ALSO BY SUSAN HAYES

## The Drift Series

Double Down

All In

Wild Card

Three of a Kind

## 3013: The Series
## (multi-author series)

3013: Renegade

3013: Stowaway

3013: Targeted

3013: Fated

3013: Scarred

## The Summoned Series

Summoned and Sold

Summoned and Stolen

Summoned and Bound